BREAKING POINT

ALEX FLINN

 HarperTempest

An Imprint of HarperCollins*Publishers*

Breaking Point

Copyright © 2002 by Alexandra Flinn

All rights reserved. No part of this book may be used or reproduced
in any manner whatsoever without written permission except in the
case of brief quotations embodied in critical articles and reviews.
Printed in the United States of America. For information address
HarperCollins Children's Books, a division of HarperCollins
Publishers, 1350 Avenue of the Americas, New York, NY 10019.

www.harperteen.com

Library of Congress Cataloging-in-Publication Data

Flinn, Alexandra.

Breaking point / Alex Flinn.

p. cm.

Summary: Fifteen-year-old Paul enters an exclusive private school
and falls under the spell of a charismatic boy who may be using him.

ISBN 0-06-623847-1 — ISBN 0-06-623848-X (lib. bdg.)

[1. Friendship—Fiction. 2. High schools—Fiction. 3. Schools—
Fiction.] I. Title.

PZ7.F6395 Bl 2002   2001039504

[Fic]—dc21CIP

AC

Typography by Alison Donalty

1 2 3 4 5 6 7 8 9 10

❖ First Edition

ACKNOWLEDGMENTS

For a talkative person like me, novel writing can never be a solitary pursuit. I would like to thank the people who listened to me babble about this book for the past year:

Joyce Sweeney, who read this manuscript twice, did an incredible amount of hand holding, and generally let me know I was on the right track;

My readers, Joan Mazza, Felizon Vidad, and Laurie Friedman, as well as the members of Joyce Sweeney's Thursday class;

Casey Burchby helped with so many details, and my agent, George Nicholson, found this novel the right home with the perfect editor.

A good editor suggests the change you've been trying to avoid and makes you glad to make them. Antonia Markiet is such an editor, and I feel lucky to know her. This book would never have happened but for Toni's recognition of this story's potential and her excellent suggestions to make this book fulfill that potential.

For my family:
Katie, my muse
Meredith, my good-luck charm
and Gene, who let me find my way

Happy birthday to me.

The metal door slams behind me. I am on the outside. Mom starts to hug me but draws back when the guard shoves my release paperwork across the desk for me to sign. Two years ago, Mom filled everything out for me. But now I am an adult—at least in the eyes of the law. Old enough to be held fully accountable for my actions.

Some people say age doesn't matter. I should have paid more for what I did, even though I was only fifteen.

Maybe they're right. But they don't know what I've paid—inside my head, where it matters.

And doing the right thing isn't always easy. Maybe it's just been too long since they were in high school. Maybe they don't remember what it was like.

Or maybe they didn't go to school with someone like Charlie Good.

CHAPTER ONE

Two Years Earlier

I was a misfit. If you'd asked me, I'd have guessed school uniforms were a good idea. Like camouflage. I'd have been kidding myself. On registration day, in my blue regulation crested polo and khakis that cleared my ankle despite fitting the week before, I knew I'd never fit in at Gate-Brickell Christian, my new school, in Miami, my new town.

I stood in the registration line, squeaking the vinylized wood gym floor against my Top-Siders. (The student handbook mandated "conservative" shoes. Also, "traditional" haircuts and "no piercings, except females, who may have one hole per ear only.") I tried to look shorter. At fifteen, I was already six one, skinny, and my dark head stuck out above the swarms of mostly blond ones. They greeted one another passionately after a long summer or, more likely, a long night. I watched them—the girls especially—trying to pretend I wasn't. A blond with glasses cornered a redhead.

"What'd you do this summer?"

The second girl, who managed to have breasts even in the hideous plaid jumpers the girls wore, shrugged. "Didn't do jack. Just vegged in Europe, then vegged here while the 'rents busted on me for wasting my youth."

The blond rolled her eyes. "I hear you."

A guy approached the blond. "Vamp 'do, Kirby."

An insult, from her reaction. Hard to tell. Their English was foreign, and I struggled to understand. Suddenly, I had the feeling I wasn't alone.

"You look confused." Someone behind me.

She meant me. I turned but said nothing.

Her hair was the best thing about her. From the rear, she could have been beautiful. Dark ringlets hung down her shoulders, gypsyish. The hair was a waste. The face, downright ugly, a screwed-up little face with eyes like raisins sunk in rice pudding, all hidden behind enormous glasses. She stared me down. She was skinny and almost as tall as I was. I realized she'd been watching me awhile. "Can you talk?" she demanded. "I mean, are you physically able to speak? I'm not being sarcastic, just curious."

I glanced around to see if anyone was listening. No one was. "I'm not confused."

"It speaks." She smiled, sort of a Mona Lisa thing she was trying for. Apparently, word hadn't reached her that she wasn't a supermodel. "You look confused. Around here, looking confused is as bad as being confused. Worse, maybe. Any sign of weakness, they eat you alive."

"Oh." Was talking to her a sign of weakness?

"I'm Binky Lopez-Nande." She stuck out her hand, sort of a weird thing to do.

I took it. "Paul Richmond." Her ridiculous name sunk in. "Binky?"

"Short for Belinda. Couldn't pronounce it when I was little, so my parents called me Binky. It's the bane of my existence."

I doubted that.

"What are you confused about, Richmond?"

"Nothing. I'm just figuring out a schedule."

"You're new here? We don't take well to newcomers unless you're someone important. Are you?" Her raisin eyes said I didn't look it.

"No. I mean, I'm going here because my mother works here." Hoping maybe that would end the conversation. Two guys my age had gotten in line behind us.

"Best reason I've heard for coming here."

"I'm trying to decide between Spanish and art." A few steps sideways, away from her, leaving only a toe in line.

"Depends. Are you college bound or running out the clock until some big trust fund kicks in?"

"Well, there's no trust fund."

"Didn't think so." A few steps toward me. "What sort of

classes did you take at your old school?"

I shuffled, considering my answer, not wanting to reveal, even to her, that there was no old school. I'd been home-schooled and felt younger than the other sophomores, despite my height. I mumbled something about moving a lot because Dad was in the army. That was true, at least. I glanced back at the two guys. They paid me no attention. Why should they? They were part of things, normal. I tried to listen in. The bigger guy, who looked like a refugee from World Wrestling Federation, with arms threatening to bulge through the bands of his uniform polo, had said something to insult his friend.

"You're a bastard, Meat," the friend said. "Know that?"

"Watch your language," the big guy—Meat—said.

His friend, even taller than me, but not clumsy, let fly a string of obscenities that would have offended a rap group. Meat took a swing. I thought they were kidding around, but next thing I knew, they were on the floor, hurtling into my knees, and I was a human missile. My nonskid shoes didn't help. My legs flew past my head, my butt hit ground. They stood, laughing, leaving me where I'd fallen. I sat a second. When I was pretty sure they'd forgotten me, I stood, edged back into line. I ignored Binky's averted eyes.

"Apologize!" A voice from nowhere.

I froze. Did he mean me? "What?"

"Not you," said the voice. I dimly recognized there was a person connected to it. Whitish hair, white chinos, white polo. He turned toward the guys, and I understood he was their leader. "Apologize to the kid."

"Aww, Charlie, we don't have to," Meat said.

The better-looking one nodded. "Not like geek-boy's going to do anything."

"Boys, boys." Charlie folded his arms. He was much shorter than his friends, but he didn't look up. Rather, they backed off to make eye contact with him. "When we crash into people, custom calls for an apology. No matter who they are." He nodded at each of them. "Meat? St. John?"

And the subject was closed. Their unison apology sounded more like a curse. They walked away, heads down.

Charlie turned to me, and I, like his friends, found myself backing to meet his eyes. They were brown, which seemed just right with his light hair. Short though he was, Charlie wasn't fat or fragile or childish like short guys usually are. Rather, he was just this small person, as if everyone else was a waste of materials. He wore sneakers—forbidden by the handbook—and his polo was nonuniform. It said WIMBLEDON TENNIS CHAMPIONSHIPS.

"Charlie Good." He didn't extend his hand. "No *E*, just plain Good."

He expected a response. "Paul Richmond."

"Word of advice, Paul. Be aware of your surroundings. You're not from around here, are you?"

I shook my head.

"Well, this can be a dangerous place. Very, very dangerous."

He smiled and walked away. Did the crowds part for him? Must have been my imagination. I turned to Binky.

"Who was that?" I asked, feeling more confused than ever.

She pulled me forward, took a card for the Spanish class and handed me one. "That's trouble."

CHAPTER TWO

Mom broke the silence in our car. "So, how was registration?"

I grunted. I didn't want to upset her. I didn't want to lie either.

"That's not an answer, Paul." Mom yanked a blond hair from her head.

I tried not to notice. I stared out the window, at the strip malls, gas stations, and convenience stores. The car's air conditioner was broken, and the humidity through the open windows pushed the air from my lungs. I felt Mom watching me. Finally I said, "The kids were sort of rich. They had Rolexes and stuff."

And she said what I'd known she'd say. "We have to try not to think about money."

She said it as we reached the parking lot for our building, a graphic reminder of the money we weren't thinking about. We parked and walked through the peeling-painted breezeways to the elevator. A sign on the bulletin board advertised FREE KITTENS, but someone had crossed out *kittens* and substituted a synonym. Mom looked away. I ripped the sign down. Mom said, "I'm sorry. I didn't want it to be like this." She pulled another hair and sighed. "I suppose everything happens for a reason, sweetheart."

"I know that." *The reason is, my father's sleeping with his secretary.* But I didn't say that, didn't even say anything about her calling me "sweetheart," which she'd promised to stop.

We reached our landing and walked in silence, me closing my eyes and praying, *Please, God. Please let us get through this one day without her crying.*

She pushed open the door. We stood there, looking at the rented beige sofa, generic table, and every stupid figurine my parents had bought during their marriage. Dad hadn't wanted mementos. He'd just wanted out. Through the still-open door, I heard a car backfiring, rap music, an argument down the hall. Mom's hand strayed to my shoulder. I backed off.

"I'll go put my books away."

She nodded, and I retreated to my room. But seconds later, as I fitted my books into the milk crates we'd decided would work for shelves, I heard her crying.

So much for prayer.

I did what I'd been thinking about doing for a while. I walked to the phone and dialed my father's number. He hadn't called since the divorce. I didn't even know what I'd say. It rang once. Twice. Three times. Then, Dad's voice on the answering machine, "You've reached the residence of Lieutenant Colonel Glenn Richmond." I hung up.

I flopped onto my bed. Mom was still crying. I wanted to go on-line, but in our tiny apartment, Mom would hear the modem, then grill me about what I'd been doing. So I lay there, breathing deeply, drowning her out from inside my head. Dad's voice was still in there too.

I couldn't pinpoint the day Dad had stopped loving us. But if I had to guess, I'd say it began when we'd moved to Kentucky and Mom started homeschooling me.

We'd moved a lot. Between kindergarten and second grade, I'd attended four schools, always transferring midyear, always the new kid being sized up by everyone. I learned to be shy. Mom was a pro at it already. By our third move, she stopped joining Bible-study groups, stopped doing volunteer work or signing me up for sports teams. I couldn't catch a ball anyway. Mom spent her days cleaning our spotless house, waiting for me to get home so we could do homework together, then curl up on the sofa and watch cartoons until Dad came home for dinner. When Dad came home for dinner.

My second-grade year, we lived in Washington. State, I think. At least, it rained a lot. Dad got home early one night, smile plastered to his face. I knew what was coming.

"Guess what?" Dad said over dinner.

"We're moving again," Mom guessed.

"Don't look so happy. I got a promotion. I'll finally be a major, and we're going to Kentucky." He grinned wider and tousled my hair. "Home of the Derby, son."

"Can I have a horse?" I asked.

"Sure." He patted my shoulder.

But Mom stood, her face a confusion of fear, fury, and despair. "Don't do that. Don't promise him things, get his hopes up like that."

"Would you calm down? It will be fun—a new adventure."

"For you, it's an adventure. For Paul and me, it's just another move, another new school, another grocery store to figure out, then move as soon as I know where the cereal is."

"The cereal?" Dad's smile disappeared like always. "This is what army families do, Laura."

"Well, I'm sick of it. *We're* sick of it."

"Can I still have a horse?" I asked.

I got sent to my room. But I heard them fighting, into the night. In the morning, I came downstairs to find that, as all warring armies eventually do, my parents had reached a treaty.

Mom patted the seat beside her. "Paul, how would you like to stay home with me? No new school, no new kids to deal with. Just you and me—together."

She'd made chocolate-chip pancakes. She always did when arguing with Dad. I loved them, though they made me sick to my stomach later. I nodded. I didn't like school anyway. But mostly, I wanted Mom and Dad to stop fighting. I wanted Mom to be happy because maybe, if Mom was happy, Dad would be happy. Maybe he'd come home more.

"Paul!" Now Mom was knocking on my bedroom door.

I jumped up. "Yeah?" It had become dark as I'd lain there.

Mom came in. She wore her ratty bathrobe, though it was still hours to bed. She shrugged. "No sense staying dressed for just the two of us." She pulled a hair.

Stop that! I wanted to scream. *Just stop it!* I didn't know whether I meant the hair-pulling or the way she'd just given up on everything. Was she doing it to torture me? And how could I keep from being a loser when *she* was so content to be one? I was through being a loser. I'd been one long enough.

She sat at the edge of the bed and motioned for me to sit too. I shook my head, but did her the favor of meeting her eyes. On the verge of tears, as usual. I knew I should feel guilty, but I didn't. I knew she was lonely. I knew she was depressed. I knew all that. But she'd been this way as long as I could remember. Too long.

But I switched on the light and sat beside her. "It will be okay," I said.

"Oh, sweetheart, I hope so." Then she was crying again. She scooted closer, wrapping her arms around my neck, reaching to stroke my hair. "I didn't want it to be like this."

"Yeah, I know." I stayed there a second, then pulled back, stood. I gestured toward the books. "I want to put this stuff away before dinner."

Over the years, the cooking had fallen to me. But today, I hadn't even started. Mom sniffled a few more times, then forced a smile. "I'll make a salad, okay?"

She didn't close the door when she left. I flopped back onto my bed, staring at the ceiling.

At first, I'd liked staying home with Mom. We'd had time for reading, going to the park, playing games, doing nothing. We went to museums and saw other kids, groups on school field trips. They formed human arm chains that tangled around the statues or Civil War relics. Instead of examining the muskets, I watched the spitball-shooting boys, giggling girls, weary moms, like they were a study I was doing.

And if it hadn't been for the Internet, the people I met in the safe anonymity of chat rooms, I'd never have known anything except what Mom thought, what she believed in. I spent more and more time on-line.

I looked at my computer again. I ached to log on now, to see who was on from my buddy list and how *their* first day of school had been, wherever they were. I'd have settled for a round of Tomb Raider. Anything to get myself out of my head. But the door was open. Mom was listening. The computer cut into "family time," which was why I liked it and why Mom hated it.

So, I just lay on the bed, stuck there with myself.

The telephone's ring startled me out of my trance. Was it Dad?

No. I hadn't left a message.

Still, I answered on the second ring.

"Faggot." A voice, a mean voice, invaded my ears.

"Go back where you belong." Another voice.

"Who is this?" I asked stupidly.

The line went dead.

I stood there, looking at the receiver, then at my own hands.

"Who was that, sweetheart?" A voice from the hall.

My mother. She'd been listening, of course. Did she know?

No, of course not.

"Just . . . just a wrong number." *Don't come in here.* "I'll be out in a sec."

"Salad's almost ready."

"Fine."

I stood and started putting away my books.

The last place we'd lived was North Carolina. I was home with Mom. Dad worked late every night, coming home long after I'd gone to bed, if he came home at all. Until, one night, he got home early. He announced he was moving out.

I gaped. Mom said nothing. Dad looked at me for once.

"This isn't your fault, Paul."

Then why say it?

"No one's fault, really. Who understands the reason for something like this?"

But the following week, we found out the reason. Her name was Stephanie—Hurricane Stephanie, Mom called her. She worked with Dad. She was pregnant.

The divorce was quick and painful, a Band-Aid ripped from a festering wound. We moved again, to Florida. But now, it was just Mom and me, and Mom had to work. She hadn't done well in the divorce. She explained that everything they owned was part of Dad's job, protected somehow. The only things Mom got were their collection of Royal Doulton figurines and me—the junk Dad hadn't wanted.

"Paul!" Mom's voice from the kitchen was trembly. *For God's sake.*

I shoved the last book into the milk crate. The telephone rang again.

I shouldn't answer. Probably another crank call.

Still, what if it *was* an obscene phone call and my mother picked it up?

Or maybe it was Dad.

"Hello?"

"That you, Richmond?"

I recognized the voice. Binky, from the registration line. "Yeah. How'd you get my number?"

"School directory."

"What's up?" *Why are you calling me?*

"Just wanted to find out your schedule. We moved here three years ago, so I know it's weird your first day."

"Is it like that for everyone?"

"Sure. Why would you be different?"

"No reason."

We talked longer, me reading her my schedule, her assuring me I'd drawn all the teachers who'd come to Gate because Principal Meeks allowed them to practice electroshock therapy or use their cat-o'-nine-tails on unruly students. But I was blown away, thinking, *I made a friend.* Maybe she was another loser like me, but she was still a friend. And that was one more than I'd ever had before.

CHAPTER THREE

"Anyone else?" Mrs. Ivins, my Algebra II teacher, looked hopefully around the room. No other hands.

I tried to sneak mine down. Too late. I was nabbed.

"Mr. Richmond." It came out a sigh.

Mrs. Ivins had begun class each day by putting a word problem on the board. They were pretty easy quadratic equations. Yet, for the third straight day, I was the only one to volunteer.

Everyone stared as I walked to the board. But a senior jock in the front row slapped my back as I passed. "Go, Richmond!"

So, I was grinning when I started.

A man can build a brick wall in 2 hours less than his coworker. Working together, they can finish in 2 hours, 24 minutes. How fast can each man do it alone?

I wrote:

	Total Time	Part in 1 Hour
Man 1	x	$\frac{1}{x}$
Man 2	$x + 2$	$\frac{1}{x+2}$
Both	$2\frac{2}{5}$	$\frac{1}{2\frac{2}{5}}$

Behind me, a snicker. Someone shushed the snickerer. Why had I volunteered? Why? I turned. Mrs. Ivins twisted to see the board. She nodded.

I wrote:

$$\frac{1}{x} + \frac{1}{x+2} = \frac{1}{2\frac{2}{5}}$$

Another snicker. *Ignore it.*

$$\frac{1}{2\frac{2}{5}} = \frac{1}{\frac{12}{5}} = 1 \div \frac{12}{5} = \frac{5}{12}$$

$$\frac{1}{x} + \frac{1}{x+2} = \frac{5}{12}$$

The room erupted in laughter. I looked at Mrs. Ivins again. She checked my work.

"Fine. Now, clear the fractions."

By the time I finished multiplying everything by the LCD, the room had calmed. I wrote the answer, $x = 4$, $x + 2 = 6$, in tiny print, then walked, head down, to my seat. I didn't look up the rest of the period. I swore never to volunteer again.

In the hallway, people still laughed when they saw me— even people who hadn't been in my class. Binky materialized through the crowd. She patted my back.

"Rough morning?" she guessed.

"You can tell that by looking?"

She held up a sheet of paper, really three big yellow Post-it notes stuck together. I read:

$x = $ I'M A HOMO

$x + 2 = $ I HAVE A HAIRY ASS

$\frac{1}{x} = $ I JERK OFF A LOT

"The jock."

"Which jock?" Binky crumpled the paper.

"When I went up to the board, some guy put it on my back." It struck me that the jock had understood the math problem, too. But he'd preferred to humiliate me.

Binky aimed and made a basket into the garbage pail. She looked at me. "Lesson one, Richmond. It might be a good idea not to let everyone know you're smarter than them. They hate that."

"I'm not smarter than anyone."

"Yeah. Trust me. You are."

Down the hall, I saw Charlie Good, the guy from the registration line. He was talking to the jock who'd humiliated me. Charlie looked up, met my eyes. He waved.

The rest of the week, I watched my back. Problem was, I'd learned about school from television. On television, when a new guy shows up, everyone wants to know him. Within an episode, he has a place in the action, some friends, a girl. Gate was nothing like that.

Wednesday, there was a foot, tangling through my ankles in social studies, tripping me. Could have been an accident. The next time, I thought maybe it wasn't. The third time, I was sure.

My locker got trashed Thursday. Someone managed to spray Coke up through the air vents. My fresh-from-the-bookstore texts were annihilated. I watched the brown liquid seep across the white pages, and I remembered being dragged to the shooting range with Dad and getting him mad by asking why they'd invented guns. Now, I understood.

Friday, whoever it was did one better, switching the combination locks so I couldn't get into my locker at all. I found the janitor scrubbing the toilets in the upstairs boys' room. Everyone called him "Old Carlos" though he wasn't much older than Mom.

"What your combination is?" Through an accent I could barely understand.

"I told you. I don't know."

Old Carlos pulled back his Florida Marlins cap, revealing his baldness. First period had started, but I needed my books. "You no got your combination?"

"Someone switched the locks."

"We give it a try. What your combination?"

No point explaining. I told him the old combination and watched him dial it. He pulled down the mechanism. The lock opened.

"It work now." Old Carlos smiled. He was missing two

teeth. "You forget, maybe."

I nodded. But I hadn't forgotten.

I was by my locker after school that same day. I'd come from the computer lab, where I killed time in chat rooms until Mom got off work. It was almost four. The breezeway was quiet. The only students left were athletes, who had practice, and me. The air was hazy, silent yellow.

Then, a voice. "Hey, faggot!"

Why did I turn? I saw a pair of white moons topping muscled legs. Then, another. And another. I looked away.

"Like that, faggot?"

I stared at my locker. The leftover drips of Coke had attracted an ant parade, swarming across the gray metal in a sugar frenzy. The three jocks left, guffawing.

"Why can't I go to public school?"

Mom was sitting in the living room, watching TV. She'd brightened when I entered, but at my question, she yanked a hair and sighed, making me sorry I'd asked.

"Lots of people go to public school," I said.

"Public schools aren't safe. I wouldn't feel right, letting you go."

"They can't be worse than Gate."

"You think that because I've protected you."

She pulled another hair.

"You don't know what's out there," she said. "Crack cocaine . . . shootings . . . gangs—"

"Those things could happen here, too."

"Please, Paul." Tears welled in her eyes. "I'd die if anything happened to you. You're all I have. Your father left us with nothing."

It wasn't her fault, I realized. I hadn't told her about the stuff that was happening. Now I tried.

"But the problem is, people are all so mean there. At least, if I went to public school, I wouldn't be the poorest kid there. The kids at Gate, they . . ."

She sighed, looked away.

I stopped. I'd been about to tell her everything, about the Coke in my locker and the locks being changed, the jock in algebra class, and getting tripped practically every time I walked into the cafeteria. But I realized she didn't want to hear about my problems. She only wanted to dissect her own.

"Never mind," I said. "It's okay."

She looked back at me and patted my arm. "Of course it is. All we need is each other." She reached to the coffee table and flicked the pulled-out hairs off her hands. She turned her back to me. "Can you rub my back, please? I'm so tired."

I didn't want to, but I reached over and did it, like always.

But inside, I was mad. Mad at her for ignoring my problems, but more than that. Mad at her for being tired. She was always tired. Tired of life, tired of work. Tired of me.

Well, I was tired too. Tired of trying to make everything okay for her. For once, I wanted to think of myself.

*   *   *   *

Later, I did the only thing I could. I called Dad again.

I got his answering machine. "Dad, it's me. I was wondering . . . if maybe I could live with you. Just during the school year or something. . . ." I sounded like a dork. "Anyway, call me back." I left the number and hung up.

That night, I waited. He had to call back. He was my father, for Christ's sake. But when the telephone rang, it was only Binky.

What kind of father would just leave me here, with Mom and this school? Could he really be that selfish?

At twelve thirty, I went to bed.

I asked Binky, "Why are people such assholes to me?"

We were eating in the shade of the oak canopy that stretched across campus. It did nothing for the heat. The suffocating feeling had settled in permanently. I'd filled my tray with food Mom would have called nonnutritive: two burgers and an oatmeal cookie sandwich. Binky had a burger too, which marked her as strange for a girl. I watched girls a lot. Most got the salad bar, which skinny Binky described as "anorexic." In the first weeks, she was still my only friend.

"Probably they figured out you're a subsidy student," she said. "That your mother works here."

"I guess so."

"This is the most expensive school in Miami, Richmond, and everyone knows it. Others have academics, sports. We have snob appeal." She extracted a pickle from her burger bun, ripped it in two, and replaced the halves on the burger. "People get emotional over who pays full price."

"That's messed up." I watched a squirrel, leaping tree to tree.

Binky shrugged. "Could be worse. At least your mom works in the office. Have you seen what they do to David Blanco? *His* mom's a lunch lady, and his father's the janitor." She pretended to shudder.

I downed the second burger in four bites. Across the way, two guys in blue caps, the kind worn by Gate's student ambassadors, looked at us, laughing. I didn't want to know what they did to David Blanco, who must have been the weird-looking guy I'd seen talking to his fat mother in the cafeteria. Or what they'd do to me. I didn't even know why I wanted to fit in with these people, but I did.

From a distance, I saw Charlie Good crossing the field. The two blue caps yelled to him, and Amanda Colbert, the mere sight of whom made my stomach flip, tried to start a conversation. But Charlie walked alone. I'd seen him often. We had no classes together, but I passed him in the halls. And I heard about him. Not by accident, but more like Charlie was a research project. What I found contradicted Binky's statement about Charlie being trouble. He seemed like the most normal person there. True, he was never fully in uniform, always wearing either contraband shorts or sneakers, always dressed in white. But his name was on last year's low honor roll, posted in a case in the breezeway, and that first Friday's newspaper carried his picture, acing his serve for match point. Charlie had made the front page.

I didn't speak to Charlie again until Thursday, second week. I was at my worst—P.E.

Soccer was invented by masochists.

I lunged, feetfirst, toward the black-and-white ball that burned on my brain like a tattoo. Up was blue, framed by a stand of oaks. Down, there were only feet. Feet, somehow making contact with that black-and-white missile as mine couldn't. Across was the goal, near but unattainable; still, yet elusive. I was inches away, running in circles. Finally, I saw an opening. The ball hit the canvas side of my Kmart sneaker and soared heavenward, carried more by wind than by my kick, crooked but straight enough. Seconds later, it hit ground, bouncing clear, no defense in sight. No one but me as it leaped toward the goal. All around, people screamed my name.

Richmond! Richmond!

I turned, faced them.

"Richmond, pay attention!" Coach Kjelson's voice rose above them. "Your side called time-out!"

But time-out was never long enough.

It started again. And again, I was in a time warp, where

nothing changes, the ball never moves, and I was always inches from glory. And as the ball slipped away, my eyes filled with watery sun, and I saw Charlie. He wore tennis whites, oblivious to the ninety-degree heat. His smile was so loud, I knew he was laughing at me. Then I heard it, ringing above the buildings. Someone slammed me into the dirt again, and when I looked up, he was gone.

I ran for the rest of the period, not even trying for the ball. That's the only good thing about soccer: You don't actually have to do anything. It was maybe five minutes, but it seemed an hour. Finally, Coach let us go, and I drifted to the locker room.

I'd stripped to my jock, inhaling the sour smell of sweat and frustration. I saw Charlie. His hair was damp from the shower. His white polo had Gate's logo; his white chinos, Ralph Lauren's. He wore his forbidden white tennis shoes. He smiled.

"You must be one hell of a student."

I stared, dumb in both senses of the word. A witty reply leaped to mind.

"Huh?"

He tilted his head back to the ceiling, not looking at me. He had no reason to remember me, yet somehow, I knew, he remembered everyone. "I said, anyone that uncoordinated must be a real brainiac."

It wasn't news, but it hurt anyway. "Whatever." I pushed

past him, not difficult. I was a giant, after all. I headed for the showers, lifted the grimy, plastic curtain, stuck my toe under the spray. His voice again.

"You always shower in your jock, Einstein?"

I jumped back, saving myself from all but a few drops, and turned to avoid his gaze. But he was gone. Still, his laughter hung in the sweaty air. The door slammed.

The next morning, I walked up the center stairway before third period. A crowd clogged the way, all staring at something hanging from the second-floor landing. People laughed and talked and didn't move an inch. I tried to shove through. Finally, when the bell rang and everyone ran for class, I saw what they'd been looking at.

The picture, taken from a calendar or something, was an obese woman, naked except for a garter belt, spread-eagle. Gross. I stared, revolted, yet unable to turn away. Across the enormous, rumpled stomach, in red marker, someone had written Blanco's Mom.

I remembered what Binky had said about David Blanco, David Blanco and me. God, what would I do if anyone did that to my mother?

For one moment, I stood there, imagining it. I wanted to hurt them.

Then, a guy's hand reached down for the picture. I heard it rip. I looked up. He was gone.

*   *   *   *

Dad hadn't returned my calls. I'd left four, maybe five, messages, and it bugged me. I mean, even if he was away, he'd have called for messages. He couldn't be this big an asshole. Then, I remembered Hurricane Stephanie. Of course. She wouldn't want me living with them. Why should she? They had a new baby. Everything was perfect. She was probably erasing the messages before Dad even got them. That night, I left another.

"Dad and Stephanie?" I paused, stupidly, like they might answer. "It's me again. Paul." One ear tuned to the hallway, to make sure Mom wasn't listening. I knew I was betraying her. "Your son, Paul. Look, if you let me live there, I won't get in the way or anything. I'll take the bus to school—whatever school's most convenient. Or walk. You wouldn't see me hardly at all. And if you need a baby-sitter for . . ." I stopped, realizing I didn't know my half brother or sister's name. ". . . for the baby, I'll do that too."

CHAPTER FOUR

The bell tower stood on the far end of campus, behind the chapel and near the athletic field. A three- or four-story structure, it stared over Gate's grounds, meant to symbolize tradition or excellence or something. Not to me. Every hour, when its bells rang, another hour of my life was gone.

Near the end of September, I walked in its shadow. Four o'clock. I kicked a rock, killing time until Mom was ready to leave. Usually, I went to the computer lab after school. I fooled around on the Internet away from Mom's eyes and ears. Sometimes, I even helped the sixth-graders with their homework because, I guess, it made me feel important that they thought I was some kind of computer genius.

But I wasn't in the mood today. Someone had made cookies in my locker. At least, it was filled with eggs and flour. I'd considered changing the lock. I didn't want to give them the satisfaction—whoever "them" was. Word of my untouchable status had traveled across campus, and now the spitballs flew so thick I sometimes ducked into the boys' room to rinse my hair between classes.

The day before, I'd asked Binky, "Why hang with me? Bet it does nothing for your image."

She snorted, probably at the idea of her having an image. "Haven't you figured it out, Richmond? I don't care what the clones think. I buck the system."

"So, I'm some project, some statement you're making?"

She rolled her eyes. "No, you're just Paul. But they can't tell me what to do."

It was a philosophy I hoped to cultivate. I wasn't having much luck yet.

The clones were out in full force that afternoon. There was a game the next day, and a pep rally. The football team was grunting. Cheerleaders were yelling pointless things, bouncing and flashing their legs in those short, blue-and-white polyester skirts and sleeveless tops where you felt you could see more if you looked hard enough. I tried not to. Why bother? Looking only made you want to touch, and that wasn't happening. I walked alone, writing a letter in my head to Dad, since he wouldn't return my calls. I felt stupid, writing him, but I had no choice. I hated Gate, hated living with Mom. Hated my life. I had to leave.

I sat on a high tree stump away from the shadowy area where mosquitoes hid. I wrote in my mind. When I reached down for my notebook and pen, I saw him.

He was about my age. He led a small, white dog on a leash. I recognized him. David Blanco, from the cafeteria and the hallway. It was the first time I'd been near enough to get a good look at him. I'd been curious since Binky had compared us, but really, I saw no similarities. Where I tried to fit in, David clearly wanted to stand out. His dark hair was bleached white, and his face bore the scars of various piercings—not allowed by Gate's dress code. His pushed-up sleeves revealed a tattoo. I couldn't make it out. The dog, on the other hand, was white and clean, brushed like he'd just come from the groomer.

What was he doing with the dog, so far away from the cottage at the back of campus where he and his parents lived?

I shook my head, imagining having to live at Gate on top of everything else.

I watched him from a distance. He walked the white fluff ball in gradually tightening circles, near the football practice field. What was he doing? Finally, the dog hunched. David whispered something to it, I couldn't hear what, then picked it up by its fluffy shoulders and put it down right in the center of the athletic field entrance. I grinned. The guy had balls, not to mention the right idea. He was making his dog crap in the exact spot where the football team would be walking in their cleats.

The dog finished its business and walked on, red ear ribbons flapping side to side. David reached to pat its head. He caught sight of me. I smiled again. David saluted and walked away.

The sermon in chapel that week was "Love Thine Enemies." I figured it would be a good idea for me to listen to that. But it was hard.

CHAPTER FIVE

"Happy teen years are overrated," Binky announced.

"What's that supposed to mean?"

"Show me someone who's cool in high school, I'll show you the unemployed guy eating double his share of hors d'oeurves at the ten-year reunion."

Being Binky's friend wasn't doing much for my social life. But then, I didn't have one anyway. So every Friday, I went over her house after school. I'd never invited her to my place. I hoped I'd never have to. Usually, we watched television. Sometimes I got to hear Binky's theories about life. She had plenty.

"Hope you're right," I said.

"I am."

We sat a few minutes, watching soaps merge into Maury Povich. Suddenly, Binky stood. "I want to show you something."

"What is it?" I was bored but too lazy to move.

"Just come on."

She took off. In a few seconds, I gave up and followed her through the empty house. She was in a hurry, nearly knocking over priceless artwork with her flying arms, me behind her. It was almost dark. Mom was picking me up in an hour. I didn't know where Binky was taking me, but I followed, across the neighbors' yards, then over a fence and into an empty, fresh-mowed lot.

"Where are we?" I dropped over the fence after her.

"We're going next door. To my church."

"That sounds fun."

"We're not going to a service, Squid. We're going to swing."

Which didn't make a whole lot of sense, either. But I had no other options, so I followed her, across the lot, over another fence, through a garden where she stopped.

"Look!" Pointing at something, nothing.

"What?"

"Don't you see?" She pointed someplace different. "There!"

"What am I looking for?"

"Hummingbird." Pointing back at the first spot.

And then I did see. Or, at least, I saw something bouncing from limb to limb, over the yellow flowers lining the fence. It moved so fast I doubted it knew where it was going. Could have been a moth, in that dim light. Or the wind. "How do you know it's a hummingbird?"

"Just do. It's here most nights, this time."

"You're here every night?"

"It's peaceful."

I'd had enough peace for a lifetime. I really wanted something besides just peace for a change. We stood, watching until the bird or whatever it was disappeared over a red-flowered tree. Binky motioned for me to follow her and, finally, we reached an old swing set crusted with leaves and spiderwebs. She brushed off a swing and sat.

"Oh," I said. "You meant swing like . . . *swing.*"

"Sure, what else? It's fun, pretending to be a little kid with no deadlines or worries, nothing serious at all. Right?"

I didn't know. I'd never been a kid like that. I flashed back—Mom pushing me on a swing at some kind of army picnic, Dad saying I wasn't a baby anymore. He'd been mad I'd placed last in the sack races. We hadn't gone the following year. But I said, "I guess."

"So, do it," she said. "Swing."

I started to. It came back to me, the pumping motion, pushing my body through the chains, legs flying ahead of me and back. Soon I was watching Binky, trying to outdo her.

But she wasn't competing. She looked like she was someplace else, someplace really flying. And as she swung, she sang softly, a sort of lilting tune, blending with the rhythm of her swinging legs.

"What are you singing?" I asked finally.

Anyone else would have stopped, caught in something so private, silly. Not Binky. She didn't care what people thought, lucky her. She kept singing until she finished.

"What is that?" I asked when she did. "Some Cuban folk song?"

She laughed. "It's a show tune."

The last thing I'd expected from her. "Where'd you learn a show tune? Thought your family was from Cuba."

She slowed a little. "My dad's family is, but they've been here a long time. *Abuelo* and *Abuelita*—my grandparents— left early. They were lucky. Sometimes, I wonder how our lives would be if they hadn't."

She paused a second, thinking about that. We both thought about it.

She said, "But Mom's family is different. They're Irish, from El Dorado, Kansas. Mom's father worked in the oil refinery. But Grandma was a beauty who tried for the Rockettes at Radio City. She'd have made it, too, except she was two inches too tall. She raised Mom on Broadway show tunes, and after Grandpa died from all the asbestos he'd inhaled at work, Grandma lived with us and raised me on them too." Binky swung higher.

I laughed at her long, stupid explanation. "So, what's the song?'

"One of Grandma's favorite swinging songs. She had songs for every occasion."

I kept looking at her. She began to swing high, singing loudly:

Buy yourself something you really don't need—
Something sweet like beautiful candy too pretty to eat.

She stopped, self-conscious, suddenly, but swung higher. "That's all I remember. I've looked for sheet music, or a tape with the rest of it, but there's nothing. It died with Grandma."

We swung in silence, me hearing the song in my head still. Finally, she said, "What do you think it means?"

"I don't know. I guess that you should try to get the best stuff, no matter what it costs." *Like Dad,* I added silently.

"Even if you don't need it?"

"I don't know. What do you think?"

She stopped pumping, slowing until her feet started hitting ground. Finally, she said, "I think the pretty apples are the poisonous ones. I think I'd rather have a plain, old Hershey bar than the most beautiful candy in the world. That's what I think." She jumped from the still-moving swing and ran, hair streaming behind her, to the church. "Come on!"

I jumped off too and followed her, past the stained-glass windows that glowed from within. She was right. About the Hershey bar, I mean. I wished I could feel that way. But I needed something else, something more. I needed some beautiful candy.

Binky led me to a side door. She pulled the handle. It didn't give.

"Locked," I said, starting back toward her house.

But she pulled harder, and it opened with a crack of peeling paint. "They leave it unlocked in case someone has spiritual needs outside normal church hours or something."

"They aren't scared of vandalism?"

"Guess they trust people."

I shook my head at this. We stepped into a small alcove that had a Bible, some used-up candles, and, of course, a collection box. Binky pushed through the door on the other side and entered the sanctuary.

I'd never been in a Catholic church. It smelled different from Protestant churches I remembered or the chapel at Gate. It smelled ancient, like candles and dust. The room glowed dull red. Binky led me around to the side, then stopped by a statue in a glass case. I could barely see in the dim light, but the case, at least, was locked. The glass looked thick. Binky crossed herself, and I barely made out that the dull, red-brown object was a wooden statue of a woman.

"What is it?" I asked.

She looked at me like I was stupid. "It's the Madonna. The Virgin Mary."

"Oh."

"It's been here forever. Someone brought it back from Spain—said the guy who sold it to him told him it was a thousand years old. They found it singing by the road."

She stopped a second, and we both listened, like it might be true. Nothing.

"He didn't believe that," she said. "Still, he bought it and brought it back here, and when it came to our church, it began to weep."

"Weep?"

"You can still see the marks on it. It wept for six days, real tears."

That was truly stupid. Probably a roof leak. These people were worshiping a roof leak. Then, I felt bad for thinking that. Gate was a Christian school. Did I believe in anything?

"There are lots of weeping Madonnas," Binky said. "They weep for the crucifixion of Christ or the sins of mankind. Some cry blood, but this one was just water. Old ladies in our church say she grants wishes, too."

I looked again. It sure was old. You could barely tell what it was, but sure enough, there were tracks of tears. And for a second, I envied Binky being able to believe in that, in anything. "Do you believe it? The wishes part, I mean?"

"You're not supposed to. The church believes in miracles, like with God, but not luck or magic or superstitions like knocking on wood. Not officially, anyway. But there are lots of superstitious people."

Which didn't answer my question. So I asked, "Have you wished on it?"

"Never had anything to wish for, really."

I shook my head. Seemed like all I'd ever done was wish, and I didn't need a statue for it.

Then, suddenly, she spun around like a little girl. She looked up at me. "But I have something now—a wish." She closed her eyes, and we stood, silent. When she opened them, she looked at me again. She smiled. She turned and planted a soft kiss on the glass cover. "Did it. Now, you."

"What'd you wish for?"

"Secret." But she kept looking at me until, finally, I closed my eyes and wished too. I knew I should wish for something important, Mom to stop crying all the time, or money, or for Dad to return my calls. Or even to be happy with who I was, with the one friend I'd ever had besides my mother. Or to believe in—something. But I closed my eyes and wished:

Please, let me make more friends. Please let me be popular.

I was ashamed of the wish. I opened my eyes and saw Binky's face, so close. *I should kiss her.* But I didn't want to. Even though I knew her wish had been about me—maybe especially because of that. Instead, I said, "Do I have to kiss the glass?" When she nodded, I did.

It was only later, sitting in Binky's family room, waiting for Mom to pick me up, that she looked at me and said, "Of course, Grandma always said, 'Be careful what you wish for. It might come true.'"

"You spend too much time with that girl," Mom said on the drive home.

At that point, I was almost ready to agree with her, but I didn't. "I only see her at school. And Fridays."

"But she calls you at home, invites you over. It's not a proper way for a young lady to conduct herself."

"We're friends."

Mom said nothing. We drove in silence, watching the neighborhood turn from . . . well, turn. . . . Finally, she said, "I suppose you're right. It's just . . . we have no time together anymore between my job and just scraping to feed ourselves. We were so close before your father did this to us."

"We're close," I said. And part of me was thinking, *God. I have one friend, and it's too much for her.* But the other part thought how easy, how easy it would be just to go back to who I'd been. Mommy's little boy. Do what she wanted and never worry.

She patted my shoulder. "I'm glad you still think so."

I shrugged her hand away. She looked wounded and yanked about three hairs at once before replacing her hand on the steering wheel.

Sometimes, I realized, I hated her. And, more than that, I hated who I was when she was there.

CHAPTER SIX

I was still calling Dad, daily now, not leaving any messages, just calling. Hoping he'd pick up. It occurred to me that he was sitting there the whole time, looking at caller ID with Stephanie. They were laughing as I called over and over. The bastard. But that would be too callous, even for him. He couldn't actually refuse to talk to his own son. Could he?

"What are you doing?"

I'd started taking walks, long ones, to fill the time between dinner and bed. The rest of my time at home, I spent on the computer.

But today, when I got home, Mom was in my room. On her knees, my hard drive and monitor on the floor beside her. She tugged on the cables.

"No!"

She looked up.

Stay calm. Don't panic.

"Don't pull that," I said. I rushed to stop her before she yanked the main plug.

She jumped. But she stopped what she was doing and looked up at me.

"It's not shut down," I said. "You can't just pull things without shutting down." Then, more to the point, "Why are you in here anyway?"

"Oh." She smiled. Actually, she looked happier than I'd seen her in a while. "I thought if we moved it to the living room, we both could use it." She found the mouse and shut down the computer. I watched the screen go black.

"Use it for what?"

"Doing my taxes. Work at home."

"God, Mom, I'll do the taxes." Hard to keep the panic from my voice. Even after weeks at Gate, the computer was my only lifeline and, more important, my escape from Mom. How could I spend hours in chat rooms or playing computer games with her standing over me, judging? "I need it for homework."

"You need it too much." She snatched up the keyboard and gestured for me to get the hard drive. I thought about disobeying, but something stopped me from openly defying her. "You spend too much time on that computer. I read about kids who waste all their time on-line, or playing those horrible, violent games. They lose touch with reality. They have no relationships with real people."

"I have no relationships anyway." She was leaving, so, helpless, I followed. "Everyone at this stupid school hates me. I have no friends. I have no—"

"You have me." She gestured toward a card table beside the TV. "I'm not saying you can't use the computer, sweetheart. I'm just saying you should at least sit with me instead of being locked in your room." She put down the keyboard and touched my shoulder.

I pulled away and dumped the hard drive onto the card table, making it sway and her scramble to keep it from toppling. I stormed into my room and picked up the monitor. I fought the urge to throw it against the wall. Amazing how she'd suddenly asserted herself when it came to thinking of ways to screw up my life. I carried the computer to the living room and dumped it on the sofa, leaving her to figure out how to hook everything back up.

"I feel sick. I'm going to bed." It was seven o'clock.

I walked around campus most days after school. Sometimes, I saw David Blanco, always near the athletic field, always with the dog. We crossed paths once.

"Hey," I said, like you say Hey to strangers you see walking, not sure they'll respond. After all, I didn't know him. I wasn't sure I wanted to.

But David said, "Hey" back, not meeting my eyes.

The dog tugged its leash.

"What's his name? The dog, I mean?"

He grinned. "Trouble." He reached to fondle its ears, and I flashed back to what Binky had said about Charlie Good. *That's trouble.*

I started to say something else, but nothing came to mind. When I looked up again, David was far away, leading the dog, Trouble, to the tennis courts this time. Through the green mesh fence covering, I caught a glimpse of Charlie himself, practicing, his blaze of white hair visible through the green. Trouble squatted.

I didn't stick around to watch, but somehow, I knew Charlie would step around it.

CHAPTER SEVEN

The word invaded my head Thursday morning. *Trouble.*
Trouble at school, trouble at home, trouble with Dad. But not
just that. Big trouble. In my brains, in my veins. I tried to
shake the feeling over breakfast, frozen waffles still hard in the
center. *Trouble is a dog.* But that wasn't it. Trouble was
coming. I knew it.

The feeling followed me to school, like a kid kicking the
seat back. It got out with me. It saw what I saw.

Though it was still early, a crowd gathered outside,
halfway between the parking lot and the main building. All
stared at the same point ahead. Some fell away, holding
mouths, closing eyes. It was something bad. I started toward
them.

"Maybe you shouldn't . . ." Mom started to say. But I was
going. She couldn't stop me, so she said, "Let me go first."

Which was stupid. I mean, I wasn't a baby anymore. Still,

the trouble trailing us almost convinced me to let her edge ahead. Nice to have Mommy to do things for me. Not this time.

"Paul, don't —"

But I was already out, and then I saw it. Trouble. It was Trouble, all right.

At first, all you noticed was his fur, clean, white like always. Then, your eyes traveled up, searching for the red-ribboned ears, bright eyes. Nothing. Nothing but flies. Someone had cut the dog's head off.

In its place, a note, written in blood, or probably just red marker:

Should have scooped.

My stomach lurched. My eyes were closed, but still, I saw them. David, the mutant, leaning to whisper to his dog, to pet it. David, walking that stupid dog around campus each day, then leading it to the athletic field, the tennis court, to do its business where it did the most damage.

Should have scooped.

When I opened my eyes, I was almost alone. The crowd around me had drifted to the main building. Then I saw why.

Old Carlos, the janitor—Mr. Blanco—stood feet away. He held a shovel and his janitor's dustpan, wiped his eyes with two grimy fingers. God, he'd been crying. Over the dog? No. Because his son would be upset. Had Dad ever cried for me?

Mom took my elbow. "Come on."

I didn't protest, glad for an excuse not to face David's father.

All morning, I waited. For something. Some horror, some sadness. Some acknowledgment that something bad had happened. Nothing. Between classes, they huddled, whispering.

Did you see?

Cool.

Gross.

Who you think did it?

Who cares?

Cool.

Serves him right.

Loser.

I almost puked.

Had it coming.

Weird.

Cool.

But no one seemed sorry or even surprised.

I met Binky for lunch in the library. It was dark in there, and my eyes hurt. We weren't really supposed to eat there, but the room was empty except for us, so no one said anything. Binky offered me a banana from her sack.

It was too sweet, overripe. I gagged and put it down, its sugary odor mixing with the library's old balloon smell. I carried it to the farthest garbage pail so I wouldn't smell it, then sat back down. "I don't get it. Some psycho decapitated a dog here. Why are they acting like nothing happened?"

Binky didn't finish chewing. "Because nothing did."

"Huh? Repeat that."

"Nothing happened." Another bite. I smelled tuna, onions, felt tears spring to my eyes.

"Nothing happened," I repeated. "So the blood, the psychotic-looking note, that was all my imagination? 'Cause I should probably go home if I'm hallucinating."

"I meant, nothing happened to them."

"How could it not have?"

"Does anyone look upset?" Mrs. Booth, the librarian, shushed her even though we were alone. Binky whispered, "David Blanco isn't one of them."

"So? Does that mean—?"

"Yes. David isn't one of them, which relieves them of having to do anything. If it was anyone else's dog, they'd have started complaining, called all the parents, investigated. People would pull their kids out of school, and everyone would be all upset."

"And that would be a bad thing? Do you know most serial killers get started killing animals?" I'd read that on-line once. "Do you know that—?"

She put two fingers to my lips, a gesture more intimate than I wanted to think about, and said, "Parents say they send their kids here for a bunch of reasons. But it adds up to one thing: They don't want to worry about their kids. Spend enough, you don't have to worry."

"And this makes them worry?"

"Not at all. It has nothing to do with them."

I couldn't begin to understand that. Binky stood, tossed her lunch bag. When I didn't get up, she turned back.

"Right or wrong, the Blancos feel blessed that the school's educating their son. So, they don't mind that the administration's also letting it get spread around that David killed the dog himself."

I stared at her, stunned. I hadn't heard that one. Finally, I said, "And you believe that?"

She shook her head. "You weren't listening, Paul."

She left seconds before the bell.

David wasn't in class that day or the next. I knew because I looked for him. When he wasn't there Monday, I went to the janitor's cottage after seventh period.

It looked more like a tool shed or guest house than any-place a family could live. Ancient coral rock with a green door so old it could give way under strong wind.

Or a hard knock. I tapped. No answer. I called, "Hello?"

The door creaked open. David stood, looking neat as ever, neater even, in his Gate uniform polo and pants. Except where there had been only scars from his various piercings, now he wore jewelry, cheek rings, earrings, nose rings, all glinting in the afternoon sun.

"What do you want?" he asked.

"I wanted to say I was sorry."

"Sorry?" The word twisted around, mocking. "For what?"

"About Trouble. I'm sorry for what happened."

"Why? Did you do it?"

"No. I mean, of course not."

"Then, don't be sorry." His mottled face was angry now. "You are the one person who should not be sorry."

"What do you mean? They didn't all do it."

"Didn't they?" He held up a hand. "You know there's a kid here who, every afternoon at three, pisses on the tile of the second-floor boys' room so my dad has to mop it before he can go home?"

That sounded crazy. "Sometimes people . . . miss."

"Every day, same time, under the sink."

I shook my head.

"And someone else leaves dead rats by the cafeteria door, mornings, for my mom to find. And someone else breaks windows here, usually in the rain. And his friend, who tears my uniform shirts in half during P.E. class. Or the other guy who . . ." David stopped, brushed hair from his eyes. ". . . who kills my dog . . . and leaves his head on my doorstep." He glanced down, red-faced, as if expecting to see it again.

"I'm sorry."

"Don't be sorry!" A shriek. He started to slam the door, slowed, and said, "You take world history?"

"Sure." Actually, I'd read it at home with Mom.

"In Nazi Germany, people who reported their neighbors to the Gestapo—were they innocent?"

"Of course not."

"How about the ones who helped Hitler gain power?"

"Um, I guess not. No. They weren't innocent." He sounded crazy. But I'd probably be the same if they'd done that to me.

"And how about the other ones, the ones who stood by, watched it? The ones who said, 'I'm not Jewish, thank God, so I don't have to worry.' Were they?"

I stared at my feet. "No. No, I guess not."

"Well, by that assessment, you're the only person here who's innocent. Everyone else—they spend their days thanking God they aren't me. If they even think about me at all."

"How do you know I don't?"

"Because you'll be next."

I didn't want to think about that. "Well," I said. "I'm sorry anyway."

"Don't worry about it. It was just another mess for my father to clean."

That week in chapel, the choir sang "By the River" and Reverend Phelps sermonized about "Whatsoever Ye Do Unto the Least of My Brothers, Ye Do Unto Me." David wasn't there. I thought about him, though. All the time. Even as I left my usual messages for my father. Maybe especially then.

When I came in from P.E. the day after I talked to him, I found my uniform shirt outside my locker on the bench. Someone had cut it in half, neatly down the middle.

I remembered what David had said: *You'll be next.*

I knew it was true.

CHAPTER EIGHT

Friday. Another pep rally after school. We were playing John the Baptist High, so all over school, cheerleaders posted signs proclaiming, BEHEAD JOHN THE BAPTIST or BAPTISM BY FIRE until Principal Meeks made Old Carlos take them down.

I didn't go. Didn't walk around campus, either. It seemed wrong, with no prospect of running into David and Trouble, so it was back to the computer lab. I didn't care what Mom said.

The trailer they used for a computer lab was the only place I felt comfortable at Gate anymore. Its hollow floors thumped and echoed when you walked. That day, it was empty, as usual. The stink of someone's lunch filled the air. Bologna. I signed in, turned on the light, chose a station away from the window. I still heard the shrieks and cheers through the walls. I logged onto AOL and scrolled through the member-created rooms. I barely heard the door open.

Whoever it was didn't stop to sign in. He walked, silent as a soldier, across the loud floors and took the station ahead of mine. I chose the Teen Truth or Dare room. I didn't look up. I didn't know anyone. I didn't want to know anyone.

Beep. From the other computer.

I kept typing.

Beeeeeep!

BEEEEEEEEEEEEEEEEEEEP! The aggravated sound of someone repeatedly pressing keys when the computer refuses to obey.

A voice. "Shit!"

I looked up, surprised. It was Charlie Good.

"Little help here?" he said.

He'd abandoned his efforts. The room was silent, except the buzz of fluorescent lights.

"I hear you're something of a computer aficionado."

"Aficionado?" Strange word. Charlie didn't even talk like other people.

"It means someone who's a devotee of something. And *devotee* means—"

"I'm okay at it."

Charlie leaned his chair back, swung first one leg, then the other onto the table, rocking at a ninety-degree angle to the floor. "Care to assist a friend?"

"With what?"

With his head, he indicated I should sit beside him. A

high-and-mighty junior talking to a sophomore. His face said this was a privilege he was granting me. Then, a raised eyebrow. Charlie's patience was wearing thin. After all, he'd invited me into his world. I should accept gratefully.

I did. I stood, wearing my enthusiasm like a slogan on a sweatshirt. "What are you doing?"

"Research paper. Guess I'm not enough of a computer geek to work this program."

For the next hour, I, Paul Richmond, sat beside Charlie Good and taught him to do computer research. A skeptic would say I did the research for him. But I wasn't a skeptic that day. If Charlie Good, for all his brilliance, couldn't formulate a query, pull up a search result, or print it out, I should help. Maybe Charlie would do something for me someday.

For the moment, I'd settle for a compliment. "Go, Einstein," he said when I—we—finished.

"Thanks." Trying not to look too pleased. I wanted to ask why he wasn't at the pep rally. But I didn't. It would be too strange.

He read my thoughts. "I sent St. John and Meat to some juvenile tribal rite. This place has too many pep rallies." He leaned forward, smiling. "Besides, I want to talk to you."

Me? But I said, "About what?"

"How do you like Gate?"

I almost laughed. "Fine."

"Liar." Charlie smiled. "You think we're all the same,

Neanderthal jocks or rich brats. Probably think I'm both. Don't deny I'm right."

I said nothing.

"But things aren't always as they seem. Someone smart as you should know that."

"I didn't say—"

"You didn't have to. I don't blame you." Charlie slammed his chair legs to the floor, his own feet following. "But you're wrong."

A roar from outside. The pep rally must have been ending. "Wrong about—"

"You think I don't know you." Charlie said. "There are things about you I couldn't possibly understand. Secret things." The outside noise had stopped, and there was just Charlie's voice and my breathing. "You think I don't know you jack off at night and wonder if you'll always be alone."

I tried not to start, tried not to let him know he was right.

He continued. "You think I don't know that your parents split up last year and, since then, you've tried to be a good son. But really, when your mother talks to you, it makes your skin crawl and you feel like, next time she touches you, pulls a hair out of her head, cries . . . you might beat her brains in."

Part of me wanted to leave. It was weird, him knowing this stuff. Creepy. Like he'd been watching me. But my eyes felt frozen to him. "How do you—?"

"Am I wrong?"

I shook my head. He gestured toward the racket at his feet. "Know why I play tennis?"

Stupid question. He was a star at tennis.

"I play because Charles Senior—my father—because Big Chuck never made the pros, so I have to. He's been teaching me since before I could walk."

"That's nice."

"Is it?" Like it was the first he'd considered it. "Guess so. Guess it's nice when someone gives you responsibility for his hopes and dreams without your permission. And it's wonderful to get out each afternoon, whether blazing sun or driving rain, and have him hit balls at me like I'm some demented golden retriever. Is it father-son bonding or indentured servitude?" He sucked his lip. "I know what Big Chuck would say. What would you say?"

I stared at the comet on the screen saver. I'd screwed up, but I didn't know how. "Why are you asking me this?"

He looked away. "Sorry. I shouldn't have. Just thought maybe you'd understand." He closed his notebook, reaching for the racket. "Guess I was wrong."

"No." I restrained myself from physically stopping him. "No. I do understand." And I did. I knew everything there was to know about trying to meet parents' impossible expectations. "But . . ."

He smiled, whirling the racket's grip between his knees. "Hmm?"

"Why are you talking to me?" I fidgeted. "I mean, people aren't knocking themselves over to be my friends."

"I just told you why."

"Oh." I guessed I hadn't heard him.

"*We're* going to be friends, Paul. That's my point. That's what I wanted to talk about." He met my eyes. "We're too much alike not to be friends."

I stared at him, and he nodded. He stood, gathered his books, the racket, and started for the door. "Go on, Paul. Your mom's waiting."

Had I offended him? I wasn't sure.

"She always leaves at four fifteen, doesn't she? It's about that now." He gestured toward the clock. Twenty after. "See you tomorrow, Paul. Before, maybe. Maybe I'll stop by."

"You know where I live?"

"I told you. I know everything."

And without saying good-bye, he left. By the time I reached the exit, there was only Mom, staring at me, all worried.

But today, for once, I didn't care.

CHAPTER NINE

That night, I thought I saw Dad. His tires skidded through the rush of dead leaves and asphalt. He was driving crazy, like Mom used to yell about. Running footsteps. Then, he was at my window.

Knock, knock, knock.

My pillow was over my head. I smelled Downy, its waves of softness lulling my brain to sleep. *Sleep.*

Knock, knock, knock. Louder.

"What?"

"Come here."

I rose, cracked open the blinds, then recoiled at his face. One side was missing, blown away. One eye stared. The other wasn't there.

"Let me in, Paul."

"But you're dead."

Through the window, streetlights glowed like cigarette

butts through taller oaks. I glanced around. I was back in my own room at our house in North Carolina. Mom was on the stairs. Had she killed him? I opened the window. A rush of silvery air. Moonlight flooded through, and Dad stepped inside. His body was unscathed. His face shone, red with blood, white with bone in the dimness.

He started to speak. It seemed a struggle, his lips barely hanging from his skull. Then, Mom was there.

"Leave us alone, Glenn. We've made a fresh start." She carried a shotgun. She clutched at me, cooing, "Sorry, sweetheart. It was him or you."

Dad shoved her aside. "He's my son too, Laura."

"I need him more. He's mine." I heard the click of the trigger.

Knock, knock, knock . . .

I opened my eyes. The room was dark. I was alone. In Miami.

Knock, knock, knock . . . "Richmond!"

"Someone left garbage out here."

"*Nice* neighborhood."

"Tell Charlie he ain't here."

The digital clock shone 1:56. I fumbled for the light, hit the lampshade. It crashed to the floor, and I stumbled across the dark room.

The face across the glass was familiar, but my two-A.M. brain couldn't place it. I registered light hair, goofy grin.

Behind him, shadowy trees, mostly burned-out streetlights. Another person.

"Charlie's waiting downstairs."

I recognized him then. Randy Meade, the guy Charlie called Meat. The taller shadow behind him, Gray St. John. Charlie's friends. Guess I dozed off again, staring at them. Meat banged the window. "Charlie's waiting."

"For what?"

Meat blew an exasperated puff of air. He looked to his friend.

"Raise a little hell." St. John laughed.

The laugh did it. It finally registered. This was real. This was happening. Still blinking in the dim light, I cranked open the window, Dad's nightmare face fading to memory. The air was hot. "I need to get dressed," I managed. In the dark, I found shorts, a T-shirt, and pulled my mystified head and trembling arms through. The whole time, I was thinking, *What do they mean? Why me?* But refusing Charlie was never an option. I shoved my feet into my still-tied Top-Siders, stole across the living room, and out the door. I didn't speak until we reached the parking lot.

"Where is he?" Still looking for a trick. The high safety lights turned shadows into monsters. I searched for Charlie's white Mercedes.

Meat raised a ham-size hand toward a black Bronco, idling with lights off. I followed, tripping across parking turds, barely getting my legs in before the car sprang to life, flinging me back into the hard leather seat. My skin, bones, organs screamed, *I'm here! I'm here!* My mouth was silent, though. And my brain, still back in bed where I thought I belonged.

We squealed out, lights still off. The driver—it was St. John—turned to Charlie, riding shotgun. "Where to?"

"Head east. And turn on the lights." Charlie handed me a bottle of something. "Welcome to the Mailbox Club, Paul."

I took a sip, a swig. The liquid burned like acid. I didn't spit it out. "What's the Mailbox Club?" When my mouth recovered.

Charlie gestured to Meat, who said, "Secret society. Started at one of the public schools, but we picked up on it."

"We perfected it," St. John corrected.

"To be a member," Meat said, "you've got to take out mailboxes."

"Take them out?" I tried another, smaller mouthful from Charlie's bottle.

"Trash 'em, knock 'em down. It's fun." Meat reached for the bottle. The lights of Kendall Drive whizzed overhead, making their faces white and black in alternating madness. I looked at Meat, then at Charlie. He met my eyes and grinned. I recognized it as a challenge.

"How many mailboxes?" I asked.

"We'll let you know when you fill the requirement," Charlie said.

I took the bottle from Meat, had another swig. Used to it, I recognized the flavor. Licorice. "What is this?" Squinting at the label in the alternating light.

"Ouzo," Charlie said. "Greek. Big Chuck and Mary took a Mediterranean cruise. I have Russian vodka and tequila from Mexico." He pronounced it *Me-hi-coh.*

"Your parents don't mind?"

"Think they know? They buy this stuff to show they're sophisticated world travelers—shots around the world sort of thing. But at home, Big Chuck sucks down Jack Daniel's, and Mary gets sloshed on daiquiris at the club." He shrugged. "They wouldn't care, though."

I nodded. The ouzo—whatever it was—had taken effect, and the light made mutilated patterns on hands, arms, legs. The heat inside and outside my body was exciting. Shapes whizzed by, outlining Charlie's face. I noticed Charlie didn't drink. That was the last thing I noticed before the night became a blur of speed, road, and ouzo.

And mailboxes. We chose a house. The mailboxes were by the curb in that neighborhood, big houses with huge yards so no one could hear what we were doing. Our intended victim, a pink dollhouse shape. Meat shoved something at me. "Come on."

I stared at the object in my hands. A baseball bat.

"Go for it," Meat said. In front, the others watched me.

"What do I do?" I looked at Charlie.

"Smash it," St. John said.

"Smash it," Meat echoed.

I still looked at Charlie, waiting. He said nothing. I thought of someone, a kid maybe, or an old person, choosing that corny mailbox, painting their number, 6870, on the side.

"Look," Charlie said. "It's no big deal. I mean, if you can't handle it . . ."

But my fingers grasped the door handle. My feet hit ground, the bat sliding out beside me. Dad had never gotten me my own bat, never took me to Little League, said I was too clumsy. I made up for it now, gripping it with both hands, using it as a battering ram against the mailbox's wooden door. Pain shot through my arms. The door barely budged. I tried again, harder. It splintered. I backed up and put the bat through the back of the box. Collapsing the sides with a half dozen swift strokes, climbing onto the truck for a better angle. I thought of Mom pulling her hair, the jocks mooning, Binky sneering, Mary weeping for the sins of mankind, Old Carlos picking up Trouble with a dustpan. I thought of Dad. All the world's power was in my bat. And in my suddenly sharp mind. The wild fire-heat around me. Streetlights danced against splintered pink wood. And I danced with them. I danced with them.

From the darkness, a voice.

"Good job. You annihilated it." It was Charlie.

I looked down at my hands, the bat. The mailbox. Charlie was right. I'd annihilated it. Only pink wooden shards hung from the stick set in the ground. I felt a twinge of something. Not guilt. Why guilt? It was a mailbox, for God's sake, only a mailbox. Easily replaced by rich people—rich bastards—who lived around here. Still, I stared at the stumpy stick. Everything had changed. Meat and St. John emerged from the truck, laughing, slapping me on the back, and whatever I'd felt disappeared. For the first time since coming to Miami— the first time ever, maybe—I belonged. Everything had changed.

"Way cool!" Meat was laughing, wasted. "Can you just picture their faces when they see it tomorrow?"

"Yeah. That'll show them." St. John crunched my shoulder, suddenly my friend too. He looked at Charlie.

I looked too. Charlie hadn't participated in the smashing, except by approving. But he'd picked me up, hadn't he? He'd *picked* me. Now, he sat, quiet, looking in my direction, but not at me. I tried to catch his eye. I couldn't. Finally, I said, "Right. We'll show them all."

I think Charlie nodded then. Hard to be sure. Meat shoved me toward the truck. I was still laughing when St. John floored the gas. Then, we were careening down Old Cutler, through sharp turns, gnarled ficus trees, past reflector lights and wooden crosses, makeshift monuments to drivers who'd bought it in knots of chrome and metal. I stared at Charlie. He didn't seem frightened by our speed, so neither was I. We were all little Charlies that night, all stoic, strong, sober despite the mercuric mouthfuls we'd swallowed, all calm and ever wise.

And there were more mailboxes to smash. Black mailboxes, white mailboxes, mailboxes with mosaic tile fronts. Or shaped like fish. Or manatees. Mailboxes that gave way to a smack of the bat and others that needed extra pressure from St. John's bumper. Even one mailbox, shaped like a plane flying on top of the world, that had to be dismantled by hand. And, through it all, Charlie watched us, faithful disciples doing his bidding. And when he said, "Enough!" I felt sad. I didn't want it to end.

"Lots of people around here have stopped buying nice mailboxes because of us," St. John said when we got into the truck that last time.

"Really?" Beside me, Meat leaned his chin on his big paw. "That's sad."

"Sad?" St. John turned to gaze at his friend. "What's sad about it?"

Meat looked from Charlie to St. John. Finally, he laughed. "Don't you know when I'm messing with you?"

St. John stopped short at an amber light, sending me into the seat back. He turned to me and said, "Meat, here, is our resident conscience. He's had a better upbringing than the rest of us losers."

"Shut up, Gray," Meat said.

"I'm just screwing with you," St. John said.

"Right," Meat said. "What's going on with Amanda? Heard she dumped your ass."

Even in the dark, I saw Meat had hit a nerve. But St. John said, "I cut her loose."

"Yeah? Saw her with Tyler the other day."

"So?"

"Had her tongue so far down his throat, I thought they'd call fire rescue."

St. John released the wheel, turned to Meat. The car swerved. For some reason, probably ouzo-related, the whole thing struck me as hysterical. I started laughing. Once started, I couldn't stop.

"Quit it." Charlie took control. I quit laughing. It wasn't hard. Suddenly, nothing was funny. "Turn the car around, St. John. This is boring."

"Right. Let's bail." St. John gained control of the car and hung a U-ey. We drove back in silence, across the highway with its neon lights, tall buildings. I was dropped off first, but in my mind, I was still with them. I don't even remember the parking lot or the stairs. I fell into bed, barely believing the night had happened.

CHAPTER TEN

Charlie didn't talk to me at school. I saw him, though, in hallways, where he met my wave with barely a lip twitch. He was usually alone. I was with Binky the next time I saw him, walking between classes, glad for once to be tall, able to see everything in the suffocating breezeway. I tried to catch Charlie's eye. He walked on.

Binky noticed, though. She looked first at me, then Charlie. That day, she wore a plastic hair clip that made her look like a Pomeranian. She raised an eyebrow. "What do you, have a crush on him?"

My head snapped back toward her. "What a stupid thing to say."

"You do." She laughed, backing away. "God, you're blushing."

I turned with a squeak of my rubber heel. I had to get away from her.

She followed me. "I was kidding, stupid. Kidding." She grabbed my arm, acting as much like a girl as possible. "I know you were spacing out." She glanced at Charlie, who'd stopped to talk to Principal Meeks. "You're not that shallow. And it's not like Charlie Perfect would notice our crowd anyway."

"Since when are you and I a crowd?" I pulled away from her. Then, at her face, I stopped. "Look, I didn't mean—"

"Forget it." She practically jogged away. I glanced again at Charlie. He smirked past Meeks's shoulder. He was only smiling at the principal. I walked alone to class.

By Wednesday, I realized Binky was right. Charlie Good wasn't my friend, not publicly at least. I wasn't any closer to the mob of friends I'd wanted. But something weird happened those days. Everyone left me alone. No locker pranks, no accidents. Nothing.

I asked Binky about it. She shrugged. "Be happy."

I tried to be. And I waited.

Without me to torment, everyone concentrated on David Blanco again. I couldn't say why I watched it. But I did. The way you look at the corpse at a funeral—as much as you try not to.

It was hard not to look at David. Since Trouble's death, he'd dyed his hair acid green and kept wearing jewelry in his piercings—violating the dress code. No one said anything, even the same teachers who got off on burning people for minor infractions like forgetting socks or wearing non-logo polo shirts. The administration probably found it easier to ignore David. I wished I could.

I noticed he carried all his books with him in a backpack, like he didn't trust them to a locker—I understood that—and one day I found him in the boy's room after lunch. He was cursing pretty loud, and I figured he didn't see me. Someone had trashed the backpack. Whatever they'd put in was on everything, grayish, gloppy, and funny-smelling, dripping off books and crusting on the corners.

David stood by the sink. He took out each book, squeegeed off the gunk with his hands, rinsed the cover, and tried to dry it. Some papers, the really bad ones, he just stared at, cursing, then threw away. He didn't acknowledge me. I chose a urinal and did what I'd come for.

He was still there when I finished. The bell rang, ending lunch. David pulled the rest of the books and shit from his backpack, muttered something about it not mattering anyway, and started for the garbage pail.

"You can't do that," I said.

He turned, like he'd just noticed he wasn't alone. "What?"

"You can't just throw those away."

"Why not?"

"Because you need them. And they cost a fortune. My mom paid, like, three hundred dollars for my books."

"Watch me." He shoved the books into the trash, through the used paper towels and down. He shoved the backpack in too. He picked up the few books he'd managed to clean and headed for the door.

"Wait," I said. And for some reason, maybe gratitude that I wasn't the one with the backpack full of crud, maybe guilt over the gratitude, I blocked his way, then fished into the trash for the gray, gloppy books. I threw them onto the counter and started squeegeeing and washing them myself.

David didn't leave. He didn't help, either. He watched me. The late bell rang, and still, I stood there, squeegeeing and washing, and getting smelly gray gunk on my shirt. I noticed it had green flecks in it too. What was this crap? Why was I doing this? Not to be friends with David Blanco. I didn't need anything to make me weirder than I already was, especially when I was almost Charlie's friend. The bell finished ringing. David stood beside me.

"Why are you doing this?" He echoed my thoughts.

I handed him a few books. "Because I'm not an asshole."

He pulled out towels and dried them. Then he took some other books and started washing and squeegeeing with me. Finally, he said, "No, I guess you're not."

He *guessed*. My shirt reeked of the crap. But I let it go. I handed him another stack of clean books. "What is this shit anyway?"

"Potatoes," he said. "This shit is potatoes."

Then I could smell it. "But where would they get potatoes?"

"Not real potatoes. Powdered potatoes, the kind they use in the cafeteria. Three or four boxes, I'd guess. Just poured them in, then filled my bag with water."

"How do you know?"

"I had a friend once who talked about a prank like this. There are chives, too—the green stuff."

I smelled it now. Gross. I wanted to get out of there, away from the stink of potatoes and chives and bathroom. But mostly, away from David, away from what I'd almost become. I wasn't that far gone. I told myself it wasn't like what he'd said about the Germans. Because David didn't want to be my friend either. I handed him the washed-off backpack, and he put his books in.

I was fifteen minutes late to class.

I opened the door. Mom stood, holding a piece of paper. "We need to talk."

Conversation had been slow around there. Afternoons I spent holed up in my room, only coming out for dinner, which I made in the slow cooker, starting at six in the morning. It had been almost two weeks since Charlie had initiated me into the Mailbox Club. He still ignored me at school. I'd gone back to calling Dad, not every night, but weird times, when I figured he wouldn't expect it. I still hated Gate, hated living with Mom.

Now, Mom held out the paper. I saw it was a telephone bill. I looked away.

"You've been calling your father," she said evenly.

I didn't answer.

She tried again. "Twenty-two calls, Paul. Twenty-two one-minute calls to his answering machine. And he hasn't called back."

"How do you know he hasn't?"

"I know, sweetheart."

I didn't need her sympathy, didn't want it. Something inside made me yell, "You don't know anything. He's called a bunch of times, but late at night. We talk all the time."

"Paul . . ."

"Just because you couldn't hold on to him doesn't mean he left *me*. It doesn't mean . . ."

I saw her restrain herself from reaching for me. "It shouldn't mean that, honey. But it does. It isn't your fault."

"Of course it's not. It's your fault. Your fault. You drove him away. He couldn't stand it anymore. He couldn't stand you anymore. And you fucked me up so bad he couldn't stand me either."

"Don't use such language."

But the word felt good, liberating. So, I repeated it. "Fuck." Then, again. And again. Because it made me someone else, someone normal and happy, someone who used words like that, like St. John. I repeated it, over and over until she walked away, wounded. Then, I was glad. And still, I kept repeating it, because that word was the only thing that kept me from crying.

CHAPTER ELEVEN

The knock didn't startle me this time.

"Give me a second," I told Meat. I put on jeans, a T-shirt. I'd laid them aside, just in case.

The ride was as wild as the first time, and I was as drunk—this time on something called Piesporter that Charlie's parents had brought from Germany. I think it was wine. I climbed into St. John's backseat after our tenth mailbox, feeling the alcohol seep through my system. Charlie said, "I'm hungry, St. John."

St. John put down his window and spat into the cooling night. "Everything's closed, Charlie. It's four A.M."

"I know that," Charlie said. He hadn't been drinking, so he sounded reasonable.

"So what—?"

"Turn here." Charlie pointed to a street we'd nearly passed. St. John veered left with a string of obscenities. A few blocks later, Charlie instructed another turn, then another into a strip-mall parking lot.

It was deserted. Abandoned cars loomed like crouching criminals. St. John glanced at Charlie but said nothing. He passed a consignment store window filled with battered strollers, a Chinese restaurant. We reached the 7-Eleven.

"See? Closed."

"Move along." Charlie flicked his hand as if brushing a speck of dust. St. John rolled forward. At the end of the line, there was a bagel place, its pink neon sign announcing B GELS. Charlie held up a hand. "Here."

"But it's—"

"I know it's closed." Charlie's voice was patience personified. "That doesn't mean we can't eat here." He gestured toward the pink-lit doorway. "See?"

I made out two images. At first, I thought they were homeless people, which Miami had plenty of. I looked closer. They were sacks filled with bagels.

"They drop them off, each morning, early," Charlie said. "They trust people to stay away out of the goodness of their hearts." Charlie looked at Meat and me for the first time. "Take them."

I started. Seemed like wine made you drunk a different way than ouzo. Drowsy, dreamy, mind barely recognizing the body's actions. Beside me, Meat said, "All of them?" When Charlie nodded, Meat said, "What'll we do with, like, three hundred bagels?"

Charlie grinned. "Question is, what will they do with *no* bagels at breakfast time?" The smile vanished. "Take them."

"Wicked." Meat laughed and shoved me at the door. I opened it, feet still heavy with sleep, wine making me powerless to resist Meat's push. I stumbled forward, found my balance, and followed Meat to the doorway. All the time, I heard Binky's words, *The pretty apples are the poisonous ones.* But that was just something she'd said because she was jealous. Smothering me, like Mom. I took another swig from the bottle I still held, somehow, reached for the bag. Heavier than it looked, its plastic caught in my fingers. I hefted it onto my back. Meat lifted his without effort. We walked to the truck. Meat hurled his bag into the cargo area, and I followed. I wondered what the storekeeper would do—for a second. Charlie reached over the seat back, and we high-fived.

"Good job, men!" Charlie said, and St. John started the car like he already knew where we were going.

"We def, we fly," St. John was singing.

"What are you, a rapper?" Meat asked, and St. John clammed up.

Next stop was the park. St. John pulled beside the playground, and he, Charlie, and Meat left the car, slamming doors because there was no one to hear. I followed, slower.

"We used to hang here as kids," Meat explained as we

pulled the bagel bags out the back door.

I thought of Binky's church, of swinging in the September humidity. But it was October, cooler.

"Now, we still party here," St. John added.

We opened the bags. Charlie pulled out smaller bags holding sesame, garlic, and pumpernickel bagels. He threw them at us. I caught one. Salt. I hated salt. Still, I kept it. "Over there." Charlie pointed to the playground. I stumbled across the patchy sand to the merry-go-round and sat. "Leave the wine in the car," Charlie had said. Meat sat beside me, then St. John on my other side. When Charlie came, he shoved between St. John and me. He'd hidden the big bagel bag in the back, then shut the tailgate. Were they as drunk as I was? Charlie wasn't, so I kept quiet, not wanting to sound stupid. In fact, we were all silent, eating our bagels, soft and gummy, still hot in the cool night. The hard salt punished my mouth, but I didn't care.

Charlie broke the silence. "Know what makes me mad?" Without waiting for an answer, he said, "If people, teachers, our parents, saw us tonight, they'd say, 'They're just a bunch of kids.'"

"We are kids," St. John said.

"Speak for yourself," Meat said. "My parents are kids compared to me."

St. John considered that. "We're old enough to drive," he said. "Old enough to screw."

I thought, briefly, of Amanda Colbert.

"Old enough to die," Meat said.

"Exactly." Charlie bit a bagel and chewed it. We all waited, in case he had something else to say. He swallowed. "Remember those kids who shot up that school? Killed, like, fourteen people. All the jocks, people who gave them a hard time." The merry-go-round swayed beneath us.

"That's screwed up," St. John said.

"Yeah," Meat said. "Weird when stuff like that happens."

Charlie said, "Yeah. Mostly because it's stuff you thought about doing yourself, taking charge like that. Taking control, making the bastards pay." He pulled out a second bagel. "Not that any of us would do it for real, of course."

"'Course not," St. John said. "But everyone acts like you might."

"'Cause we're young," Meat said.

"We're shit," St. John said.

"Shit," I echoed, because I hadn't said anything yet.

Charlie threw his bagel in the sand beneath us. "I'm so sick of that. The so-called adults. Think they know it all with their questions." He clasped his hands together, looking for all the world like my mother. "Charlie, angel, you don't know anyone with a gun, do you? Do you ever feel angry, honey? Do you ever feel misunderstood?" He turned to me. "Well, do you, Paul?"

I started. The merry-go-round squealed. St. John and

Meat laughed. Finally, I said, "I don't know."

"Don't you, Paul?"

"Don't you, Paul?" St. John echoed.

"Don't you, Paul?" Meat, with a giggle.

Charlie said, "Sure you do, Paul." He patted my shoulder. "How could you not? The so-called adults don't understand, do they? They don't understand about honor. They don't understand about loving your friends, about taking care of one another."

I looked at Charlie. Then, Meat and St. John, a tall shape and a bulky one. Were they my friends? I mean, they never even talked to me at school. Yet Charlie spoke of friendship, love even. And here they were including me, letting me be part of this night. This incredible night.

"Right," I said.

"They aren't like us," Meat said.

"Right. That's why I get mad when you two bicker like children." Charlie gestured toward St. John and Meat. "Or when Einstein here acts like a scared little boy getting to play with the big kids. 'Cause we have to stick together, have to be loyal, respect one another. Have to take control."

"'Cause everyone thinks we're scum," Meat said.

"They don't know better," Charlie said.

"But we do, right?" St. John said.

I turned, feeling Charlie's closeness. He nodded. "Right, Paul?"

I shifted. Why was Charlie putting me on the spot? But I said, "Right."

Before I'd turned to Charlie, I'd been watching down the street. Now, I looked back. A car. A police cruiser, lights off. It curled around the outer edge of the park, closer and closer. Finally, it pulled beside St. John's truck and stopped.

"Shit," St. John whispered. I felt something like a foot to my stomach.

"Be cool." Charlie's eyes narrowed.

The door opened. The cop stepped out, a short, muscular guy, the kind who became a cop so he could have authority over someone. Like guys Dad knew in the army. Or Dad.

"Morning, boys."

"Morning, Officer." Charlie, who was sober, stood.

The cop eyed us. "I *said,* good morning, boys."

I shifted an arm on the cold, metal bar and said, "Good morning, Officer" with the others. The merry-go-round squeaked. Would they call my mother? I'd rather just die in jail.

The cop came closer, walking chest-out. "What are you boys doing out this time of night?"

Again, Charlie picked up the slack. "Waiting for sunrise, sir, reliving childhood memories." He gestured toward the merry-go-round. "It's not a school night, sir."

"Little breakfast, I see?" The cop gestured toward the bagels, just a small bag. The others were hidden.

"Yes, sir. Care for one?" Charlie—how could he be so cool?—Charlie reached for the bag by St. John's feet.

The cop stiffened, like he thought Charlie might go for a weapon, then relaxed. "No, thanks." I heard the grit of sand under my shoes, the sound of night insects, and watched, mesmerized, the strobing light on his squad car, turning, turning. The cop turned on his flashlight, shone it on St. John's truck. "This your car, son?"

Charlie nudged St. John, who said, "It's mine."

"Mind if I have a look?" Without waiting for an answer, the cop walked closer.

Oh, God. All those bagels. If he saw them . . .

"I wouldn't, if I were you," Charlie said.

The cop turned back, smirking, letting his light shine in Charlie's face. "You wouldn't, would you?"

How did Charlie keep from moving, squinting? A mosquito buzzed my ear, but I didn't dare swat it. Charlie said, "You have no warrant, have you, to search his truck?" Charlie's voice stayed cool. "We're nowhere near it—certainly not close enough to grab any weapons. We present no danger. We're not stoned or anything. We definitely haven't given our permission. What would happen if someone investigated this search?"

"What do you know about it?" But the cop moved away from the truck, toward us. It dawned on me that Charlie knew something about the law, somehow. And the cop was listening.

"Plenty." Charlie didn't move. "My mom's a U.S. attorney, Mary Good—no *E*. Works in Washington, mostly. Her specialty's prosecuting cops who do bad searches."

The cop didn't move. I stopped picturing Mom pulling her hair.

"Don't think she'd look kindly on you harassing her son." Charlie shrugged. "You know how moms are."

The cop shrugged too. "Hey, I wasn't going to search the car."

Charlie smiled, understanding. "Didn't think so."

"But you're not supposed to be in the park this time of night." With his flashlight, the cop lit the sign posting park hours.

"Oh, is that all?" Charlie stood, gesturing for us to do the same. "Well, men, we'd best leave, then." I followed, barely finding my feet beneath me. "Thanks for the advice, Officer . . ." Charlie squinted at the cop's badge.

"Wolofsky," the cop said.

We piled into the car, managing not to break up for a block or so. Charlie sat, trancelike, saying, "Keep a cool head. That's what Big Chuck says." Then, Meat started to giggle. St. John followed, a full, hollow laugh. Not me. I watched the fading streetlights, the roadside benches flashing by, the Dumpster where we threw the uneaten bagels, and I knew that with Charlie, I was safe. Charlie could get away with anything.

* * * *

Monday in chapel, the sermon was "Thou Shalt Not Steal." I couldn't help but glance at Charlie when Reverend Phelps announced the topic. He sat, hands in lap, listening like the perfect Christian schoolboy. Maybe he even was.

CHAPTER TWELVE

"Write about a childhood memory," my English teacher had said, probably thinking she was being profound. Thinking that it would be easy, anyway. Miss Bundy, who reeked of CK cologne and drove a new white Saab her parents had probably bought, couldn't have imagined childhood would be a difficult subject for anyone. But it was for me. Oh, I knew what the clones would write: "My First Bicycle" or "Our Third Trip to Europe." But my childhood stretched behind like so many identical calendar squares. Read with Mom, watched television, wished Dad would come home, then regretted it when he did. Nothing ever happened. At least, nothing memorable. Nothing memorable had happened until this month. Until Charlie.

Maybe, I thought giddily, I could write about smashing mailboxes or stealing bagels. That would be an A paper, all right.

I calmed myself.

I stared out the window, flipping through memories like tabs on a notebook. All I remembered was trying to keep Mom happy, keep my parents from fighting.

Finally, I wrote about going to Disney World when I was five. I could be a clone, too.

"When I walked into class, everyone turned to stare. Then, they looked away."

Amanda was reading her English essay. I fidgeted, suddenly uncomfortable in my clothes.

"I was nine, and it was my fourth school."

Beautiful. Perfect. Hot. Adjectives hit my ears like enemy missiles, then fell away, harmless. Roget himself couldn't have come up with a word for Amanda Colbert.

"Every year, Dad promised we were somewhere to stay. But every September, there I was, staring at the linoleum. Different schools, same sinking feeling."

Amanda sat three seats behind me. Impossible angle. Still, I strained to watch. She'd never read in class before. I couldn't remember hearing her voice. Now, her eyes didn't leave the paper. Her reddish hair fluttered across her forehead, obscuring her face. She didn't fix it. She was scared. Suddenly, the feelings I'd been having for girls in general since coming to Gate all concentrated themselves on one girl. This girl. This girl was different. This girl was real.

This girl was Gray St. John's ex-girlfriend. He still liked

her, Meat had said. She might as well have a sign hanging around her neck: LOOK, DON'T TOUCH.

Still, I watched. She kept reading, about sitting alone at lunch, crying in her pillow every night. "I thought I'd never make friends," she said.

I know what Binky would have said. *Poor baby. Such a deprived childhood.* But me, I longed to reach back through the years and comfort her. I'd been there too.

She looked up and met my eyes. A second, no more. It meant nothing. But she smiled.

I forced my eyes down to my paper.

I was still recovering from the Great Bagel Caper when Charlie sent another shock wave. Friday morning, I fumbled through my books, mentally preparing for the exhilarating change from religion to Algebra II. Down the hall, Mr. Motter talked to Miss Bundy. A jock named Pierre, one of the guys who'd mooned me the first week, grabbed Emily's lacrosse stick, making like he'd hook Motter's toupee. The assembled clones cheered. Motter walked on, oblivious. Charlie emerged from the mob.

He leaned against my locker. "You free after school?"

He wanted more homework help. Still, I said, "The usual." Not mentioning that the usual was going over to Binky's house.

"Blow it off," Charlie said. "We should hook up after

school. You could come over my house." Charlie was already looking elsewhere.

"Sure." I glanced around. Did anyone else see us talking? Yes. Down the hall, Binky frowned. I met her eyes, then looked back at Charlie. "Are St. John and Meat—?"

"No, just you. I'm not a pack animal." He shifted his book bag. "If you can."

He walked away. Binky was still standing, watching us. When Charlie left, she came over.

"What were you talking to *him* about?"

"Nothing. I mean, he had a question about the assignment—he's in my Algebra II class." Did she know I was lying? That Charlie was in none of my classes?

She did. I was sure. But she said, "Oh."

"I need to get to class."

Binky smiled. "Algebra, right? The one Charlie Good's in with you."

I shifted foot to foot. "Yeah, well, he transferred in."

"Whatever." She shrugged. "See you after school, then?"

"Can't." Shifting faster, desperate to get away. "I've got stuff, family stuff."

"Next week, then."

She started toward Motter's room, then turned and waved. I waved back and went in the opposite direction. But somehow I knew I wouldn't be visiting Binky's house next week or ever again.

CHAPTER THIRTEEN

Later, we pulled into Charlie's driveway in his Mercedes. My first ride, and I was shotgun.

I crossed the threshold, eyes open, looking for something but not sure what. Something to explain what made Charlie—well, Charlie. Yet, the house, though rich and beautiful, was ordinary. Beige. The right number of books on the correct number of shelves. Even the pool, surrounded by palms through the French doors, was typical around there. The tennis court occupied the prized spot beside it. Nothing was surprising, and that surprised me. I'd expected Charlie's world to be painted in colors I'd never seen before. Not beige. Anything but beige.

"Hey. Anyone there?" Charlie interrupted my thoughts. I jumped. "Sometimes, you look like you're curing cancer, Einstein."

"Nothing like that." My eyes fell on a framed photo,

Charlie under a banner for the Junior Orange Bowl tennis tournament. "That's your dad with you?" He didn't look like Charlie, but he had his hand on Charlie's shoulder.

"The man himself."

Charlie didn't smile. "Sorry," I said. "What were you—?"

"My room's upstairs."

I followed, still blown away about being there. The first thing I noticed was the computer. Couldn't help it. It was a new Dell, with flat-screen monitor and speakers I'd have killed for. Before I knew it, I was touching it. I saw Charlie looking and backed off. "Wow. Some setup."

"Is it?" Charlie shrugged. "Birthday present."

"What kind of software do you have?"

"You're sure into computers." But he smiled and flipped on the stereo. Someone's drum solo filled the air really loud, so I knew we were alone. Charlie sat on the floor. "Turn it on and look," he yelled.

I sat on his desk chair—leather soft as flannel—and fired up the computer. I scrolled through the programs. He had everything. He had Doom II, which Mom had forbidden once she'd seen Doom. And all the Tomb Raiders—Lara was hot. I pointed to Doom II. "Where's the disc for that?"

He gestured toward the CD rack. "I have Quake III Arena too."

I nodded. There wasn't even time to look at everything.

"And The Last Revelation. But mostly, I use it for

homework. Like word processing."

I nodded.

"Play on the Web sometimes, especially since last year's honors awards. Meeks's keynote address was about the 'Influence of the Internet on our children.'" He said the last part in Meeks's lispy voice.

I laughed. "What'd he say?"

With his other foot, Charlie removed one whitish Top-Sider and kicked it to the floor. He wore no socks. Gate required them. "He's against it. Misses the old days when they communicated by Morse code."

I laughed again. "Or Pony Express."

"Sent Mary scurrying for the parental controls, though," he said.

"Yeah, my mom did that too."

"I told her I'm not that easily influenced, and she respected that." He kicked the other shoe aside, wiggling his toes. "It didn't block much anyway. Mostly porn sites, and who cares about that?" I nodded, though I wouldn't have minded seeing one. Charlie reached for the volume knob, turned down the stereo. "Found some wicked websites, though. Pranks, stuff to do to people. Pretty wild."

"Like what?" God, I still couldn't believe I was there.

"One funny one was putting birdseed on someone's car. Makes the birds come and crap all over it." He grinned. "Haven't done that one yet. Saving it for someone special."

I laughed, picturing it. "What else?"

He leaned on his elbow, starting to tell me. Then, a voice from the hall.

"Charlie!"

I started. Charlie sprang to a seated position, feet to floor, hunting for his discarded shoes. "In here, Dad." He rolled his eyes, mumbling, "Don't you ever work?"

Like Charlie, Mr. Good wore white—shorts, polo, tennis shoes. Actually, he was dressed for tennis. Charlie stood, still shuffling into his shoes. I stood too. Charlie's Dad snapped off the stereo. "What's this?" Walking closer, next to Charlie.

"Dad." Charlie stepped back. "This is Paul Richmond. From school."

"Forget something?" He took my hand, looking only at Charlie. "Good to meet you, Phil."

"Oh." Charlie stared at his shoes.

"Now he remembers." Charlie's father smiled at me, like we were coconspirators against Charlie. "Pretty hard to forget a practice we discussed this morning."

"Thought it was later."

"*Should* we start later?" He dropped my hand and turned full attention on Charlie. "You tell me. Your backhand was for shit Saturday." His posture was straight, military. He was much taller than Charlie and bore down on him. "That little Chicano kid almost beat you."

Charlie backed away. "Dan's not a Chicano, Dad. He's

Colombian. And he was born—"

"I don't need his life story." Charlie's dad stepped closer. "He almost won. Five sets. The last one was seven–six."

"He's two years older, Dad. He's in college."

"Are there age divisions in the pros?"

Charlie turned away. "Guess not."

"You guess?"

"No, sir. There aren't."

"Better. And look at people when you speak. Eye contact. You look like a punk."

"Yes, sir." Charlie gestured at me.

Mr. Good remembered I was there. "I apologize, Phil. My son needs to get his priorities straight." He turned back to Charlie. "See him to the door."

"Yes, sir."

I stared at Charlie. He was my ride, after all. He wasn't saying anything, though, just walked to the door. Was I supposed to stay until he finished? Wait outside like a dog? Finally, I said, "Um, that's fine, sir. But Charlie drove me here. I don't . . ."

Mr. Good raised an eyebrow, as unaccustomed to being disagreed with as I was to disagreeing. Then, a smile, quick and blinding as Charlie's. "Of course. Rosita can drive you home." He nodded at Charlie. "Two minutes."

"Yes, sir," Charlie said for the third time.

"Good meeting you, Phil."

"It's Paul," I said, finally. But Mr. Good had already left.

I gathered my stuff while Charlie put on tennis shoes and socks. He walked me to the kitchen. Who was Rosita? The maid, I guessed. I didn't ask. The house was silent, and so was Charlie. The kitchen had a cabinet in the center, with pots and pans dangling lethally from the ceiling. Charlie stopped under them, turned to me. "My father." He stubbed his shoe against the peach-colored tile. "My father's a little . . ." The word *crazy* hung in the air, but Charlie said, "See, I'm ranked in the state, and he thinks I'm good enough . . . I could go all the way, skip college, go pro. Like Jennifer Capriati. Ever hear of her?"

The name was vaguely familiar. I nodded.

"She grew up around here. She's on the pro tour now. Anyway, Dad, he has me in all these junior tournaments, the JOB, Fiesta Bowl, even flying to Australia—my whole Christmas break. He thinks I can qualify for pro tournaments by senior year. If I work hard enough. I'm good enough, too. From there . . ."

"That's great." But not surprising. Charlie excelled at everything, after all.

"I'm good enough to do it, but I'm lazy. Too many outside interests, my dad says. I need to work on just tennis. I need to." He'd slipped away, not talking to me anymore, but to himself. "I have a private coach, but that's not enough. It's not enough. That's why Dad takes off work to coach me. I'm damn lucky he can do that, right?" Charlie glanced outside. I looked too. Across the pool, Mr. Good bounced a ball with his racket on the blazing green court. He nodded at Charlie, then his watch. "Takes practice, though, perseverance, Dad says. Live to win. Win. Win." Punching his thigh with each repetition of the word. "We're very close." He smiled, looking out again. "I'm really lucky."

"Sure."

A woman, it must have been Rosita, came in. She was beautiful, the buttons of her white uniform almost popping over her tanned breasts. I couldn't help staring. Even the help was perfect here. Charlie said something in Spanish, explaining I needed a ride, I guessed, and where I lived because I heard the word *Kendall*. She went for the keys. Charlie glanced outside. "You okay here? Can't keep Big Chuck waiting."

I nodded, and he left. I slouched against the counter, waiting for Rosita.

Charlie walked past the pool, across the trimmed grass, grim as a soldier. But when he stepped onto the court, he smiled and hit his father's serve dead-on. They volleyed, Charlie lulling Big Chuck into a false sense of security with easy back-line shots, then suddenly smashing the ball barely over the net, out of reach. The yellow ball caught sunlight against blue sky. And I wanted to be Charlie as much as ever.

CHAPTER FOURTEEN

It was starting to piss me off that Charlie ignored me at school. Like Thursday, I passed him near the library. He didn't acknowledge me. Binky had been expounding on her theory of why Motter's toupee looked different, days it rained. When I glanced at Charlie, she stopped.

"You don't really want to be friends with him, you know."

"Right." Then, I remembered myself and said, "With who?"

"Charlie Perfect." Smirking at my discomfort. "He doesn't have any real friends, just hangers-on. Stooges." She turned and stared at Charlie's back. He was out of uniform, as usual, in white shorts. "He hung with David Blanco last year, and you can see where that's gotten him."

I stopped. "David Blanco?" Then, "No, he didn't."

Binky shrugged. "Must have imagined it."

She started on Motter's toupee again. I nodded, barely

listening. Maybe I even laughed. She was usually pretty funny. But it bugged me. Why would Charlie have been friends with David, then me? Was it some kind of goof he pulled—take a loser to lunch?

Charlie was in the computer lab that afternoon. I tried to ignore him. I started to sit in back, saying nothing. Before my butt hit the seat, he turned toward me.

"Hey, Einstein." He smiled like usual. With his hand, he beckoned me over. I didn't want to go. Yet it was like he had a remote control.

"Another research project you need me to do?" I said, trying to sound ironic.

Charlie didn't pick up on it. "No, just screwing around on-line."

I came closer, close enough to see the icons across the top. He clicked the X in the corner, closing the window before I could read the screen.

"What, like a chat room?"

"Chat rooms are for losers." He gestured toward the chair by his. "Incredible stuff on the Web, like I said." He closed his pen, one of those expensive ones you close by twirling. "How can I help you, Paul?"

I didn't sit. "You're the one who called me over."

"So I was." He frowned at the empty seat. "Hadn't thought it was against your will."

"No." Still standing, but edging toward the chair. "It wasn't." The chair hit my calves. I backed into it.

"You've been smiling and waving all week, Paul."

You haven't waved back. But I didn't say it. It seemed petty. "I wasn't sure you saw me."

"I saw you." He smiled now, beatific. "I told you the first day, it's important to be aware of your surroundings."

"Then why—?"

"Why is it so important I wave in the hallways?"

"Why's it important?" I looked at my hands. "'Cause everyone thinks I'm a dork with no friends."

He stared at me. There was the click of the wall clock, advancing a minute, the racket of the AC. Finally, Charlie's voice.

"I'm disappointed, Paul."

And he looked disappointed. I stared at my hands harder.

"I thought you liked me, Paul. I don't invite just anyone to my home. But now, I find out you only want to impress people."

"That's not it."

"What then?"

I wanted to ask him about what Binky had said, about David Blanco. But I didn't. Instead, I said, "We're friends, like, one day a week. Other times, you act like I'm a leper."

"Surely not." He removed the pen, studied it. "I don't hang with many people, Paul. I'm not a crowd person." The gold pen gleamed as he twirled it in his small fingers.

"I see you with Meat and St. John sometimes," I said.

"St. John and Meat have proven their loyalty time and again. You, I'm less sure of."

"What do you mean?"

"Here you are, saying, 'Make me cool, Charlie. Elevate my miserable status.' Why should I? What have you done for me besides want something?"

What about the nights of the Mailbox Club, the risks I'd taken?

"I just thought we were friends," I said.

"We are friends. I told you we were." Charlie smiled, finally, charitable. "It's just, you want more. I can't give you that right now. I really don't know you that well."

That was true, I guessed. I wanted a best friend, someone to hang with all the time. I'd always been alone before. Maybe I didn't know how to act with a friend? So I said, "What would I have to do? To prove I'm loyal?"

The AC ground to a stop. Silence. Charlie replaced the pen behind his ear.

Finally, he said, "Well, there is one thing."

"What?"

"Your mother works here, right? In the office?"

He knew that, I knew. "Right."

"So she has keys and stuff?"

I nodded. What did Mom have to do with anything?

"And you're some kind of computer genius, right?"

"I wouldn't exactly say . . ."

Tipping his head to one side. "Don't be modest."

"Okay, maybe." But thinking, *Yeah, I'm pretty smart,* wanting to show off.

He looked toward the closed door. There was no noise outside, like anyone walking by could hear us. Charlie said, "See, I got a D in biology last semester, Zaller's class. All A's and one D. She had it in for me."

I nodded.

"I changed it on my report card so Big Chuck wouldn't freak. He freaks about that stuff."

I nodded again, thrilled to be in his confidence.

"Change it."

"What?" I glanced at the door, even though I knew it was closed. "How would—?"

"Log on to the school computer and change it."

I almost laughed. It was like a movie, computer hackers or something. But Charlie was serious. He'd seen the same movies. Finally, he said, "Should've known you wouldn't."

He was serious. I wanted to do what he asked. He'd done so much for me, including me with his friends, having me over his house. Things he didn't have to do. And there was the promise of more, of being his friend and really belonging for the first time in my life. I wanted that more than anything, enough to do *almost* anything. But still . . .

"It's just . . . my mom would get fired if I was caught. I'd be expelled."

"And we could have been arrested the other night, but we weren't. I saw to it. I took care of my friends."

That stopped me a second. I faced him. He seemed so disappointed, disappointed in me. And I remembered his father. I could tell it was important to Charlie to please Big Chuck. I understood that miserable feeling. I wanted to say yes, but I couldn't. Pranks were one thing. This was the big leagues. I just wasn't that kind of person. I glanced away. "Sorry."

I couldn't look at him, but I couldn't leave, either. I listened to him rolling the mouse around, jiggling it just to keep the screen from blanking out. "Sorry," I repeated.

"It's fine."

"It is?" Still not daring to look.

"Sure." He stopped jiggling. "Isn't it time you left?"

I looked. Quarter after exactly. Maybe he wasn't angry. He must have known his request was outrageous, probably expected me to say no. Maybe it was even some sort of test. I managed a glance. He was smiling. "See you around?" I asked.

"Sure." Turning back to the computer. "'Bye now."

He kept smiling. I didn't—couldn't—look back. Just gathered my books and left before his smile faded.

The next day, Friday, I made my way across the gray and brown locker room after P.E. I hated volleyball even more than soccer. I'd been hit twice in the face, a personal worst even for me. The second time, I was sure the server, Pierre, had aimed at me. That hadn't happened in weeks.

I twirled the combination lock, flung open my locker. Empty. After glancing around for the uniform polo and khakis I knew I wouldn't find, I sat on the bench, contemplating the prospect of three years at Gate. I'd been so near the pinnacle, and I'd thrown it away. Now, Charlie had thrown me away. I sat the rest of the afternoon, P.E. classes going in and out. I knew I should go out in my P.E. clothes. I'd get in trouble for missing sixth and seventh periods. I didn't care. The final bell rang. I walked to the library. An hour later, I rode home, ignoring Mom's questions. I went to bed.

Charlie didn't come by, of course. So, I spent most of the weekend ignoring Mom and wondering what Charlie and his real friends were doing. But Sunday morning, Mom looked out the window.

"Oh my goodness," she said.

"What?" I glanced away from the television. Mom and I had been getting along all right, because we weren't talking much. This time, her freaked-out tone caught my attention.

She kept looking ahead. "There are birds all over our car."

I didn't need to look, but I did. We ran downstairs, past the car wash station and the makeshift basketball hoop that swarmed with neighbor kids laughing and yelling in their private language, neither English nor Spanish. We reached the car. It was covered in birds, bird shit. Birdseed. I put my arm around Mom's shoulders and promised to wax the car.

It was then I faced my mistake. I'd offended Charlie. That wasn't something you did.

But I wasn't mad at Charlie. I was mad at myself for not appreciating what I had.

Monday's sermon was "How the Holy Spirit Convicts Abusers of Power." I wondered if anyone at Gate even *noticed* what Phelps was talking about. Or was he just up there talking to himself—and maybe to me?

CHAPTER FIFTEEN

"Dad?"

"Who is this?"

I hadn't had the nerve to call him at work. When he'd lived with us, he'd forbidden us to bother him there. He'd said it was because his work was important. He had no time for small talk. He'd probably been out with Stephanie. Or on his desk with her. Now, I called him at work. I'd figured he couldn't tell his new secretary not to put his son's calls through. I'd figured right.

"Dad, it's me. Paul."

"What is it?"

"Have you gotten my calls, my letters?"

"Yes."

"Well, can I—?"

"It's not a good idea, Paul."

"What do you mean?"

"Just what I said. It's a bad idea."

"But you don't understand. You don't know how it is here, how mean everyone is. How much I hate . . ." I stopped. Ever since what happened with Charlie, it had become important again to move out. School was terrible. Home was worse. I didn't want to betray Mom by saying how I hated living with her. But how else could I convince Dad?

He didn't let me finish anyway. "I can't talk now."

"Then when?"

"Look, can't you take a hint?"

"What?" Sure I'd heard him wrong.

"You're a smart kid. Take a hint. You can't live with us. I was trying to spare your feelings, but there it is. You wouldn't fit in here."

"But—"

The line went dead.

I held the phone until the operator came on saying, "If you'd like to make a call, please hang up and dial again. If you need help . . ." Gently, she said it. Three times, gently before attacking my ears.

I needed help. But not from the operator. I slammed the phone down and went downstairs and out the guard gate before even realizing what I was doing. I sat on the curb, my legs resting in Kendall Drive with cars swerving to avoid them. I didn't care. Every one of those cars had someplace to go, someone to go to. Everyone but me. I had only Mom crying and clinging, needing me to do everything for her. Dad, who'd found someone else. People at school, who laughed at me.

And Charlie.

And suddenly, Charlie's request didn't seem unreasonable. Not at all. Why had I thought it was a big deal? It was a victimless crime, really, changing a grade. If there was a victim, it was the school. And I hated the school and everyone there.

Charlie would protect me from them. Charlie was strong and would make me strong by association. Changing the grade seemed almost too little to do in return. No wonder Charlie was mad. No wonder he expected loyalty. He was the only one who'd been loyal to me.

It was almost dark, and the distance between cars had lengthened. I took a pebble from the roadside, threw it across the lane. It hit an eastbound car. The driver honked. I didn't care.

I don't know how long I sat there. Long enough for Mom to look panicked when I came in. She started to talk, but I passed her without a word. She was a stranger to me. I went to my room and punched in the number I realized I'd been dialing in my head for more than a week. Not Dad's number. Never Dad's number again.

When Charlie answered, I said, "I'll do it."

"Good man," came his reply.

And I smiled. It felt great to be back on Charlie's good side.

CHAPTER SIXTEEN

Finding Mom's key was the easy part. I'd scoped it out before I'd even agreed to Charlie's plan, because maybe I'd always known I'd do it. It was on her key chain, between her car key and keys to our three front-door locks. Taking it without her noticing was another matter.

As usual, Charlie had the answer. "Get it Friday, when she won't need it all weekend. Then, copy it before she notices it's gone."

We'd been screwing around on the computer in Charlie's room. First, we were playing Quake III Arena. Then, Charlie said he'd heard of a website with secrets on how to get to the next level, so we looked for that. But it had nothing we didn't already know. I'd been at Charlie's house every day that week—not doing his work, either. We'd just been hanging, like friends. Like best friends.

"She notices everything." I rolled my eyes. "Besides, it's

one of those keys you can't copy."

"Ah. School security measures." Charlie started down to the kitchen. I followed him. He rummaged through a drawer. I tried not to watch over his shoulder. I mean, it was a junk drawer, nothing special. Like our junk drawer at home. He found what he wanted. "Like this?" Holding up a Medeco key. When I nodded, he handed it to me. "Okay. Switch it for the one on her key chain. We'll do the deed Saturday, and switch them back before she needs hers."

It would work, I realized. Yet, I felt something in my stomach. A twinge. Like someone had tickled my insides with barbed wire.

Binky was mad at me. Ever since I'd told Charlie I'd do what he wanted, he'd been including me in his group at lunch. So now, I had all these friends, even girls. Binky ate alone. I felt bad about that. But was that my responsibility?

Thursday, I found her in the second-floor breezeway. Lunch was nearly over, and people were hanging by lockers, pretending they might cut afternoon classes or it didn't matter whether they went or not. Except Binky. She had a book propped inside her locker, reading. I glanced at it. Sartre. Not assigned reading, either.

"Hey," I said. "Good book?"

"It's a play, *No Exit*. I've read it a bunch of times." She closed the book, then the locker and twisted the combination-lock dial. "The thesis is, Hell is other people."

"Oh."

"Missed you at lunch."

It was an accusation. I squirmed, glanced down the hall. A bunch of jocks were screwing around by the water fountain. One waved. I nodded at him. Binky smirked. "What's wrong?" I asked her.

"Oh—nothing."

She was mad all right. And suddenly, I was mad at her for being mad. Why should she be? She'd do the same, in my situation. "Can't I have lunch with someone else once?"

"Who said you couldn't?" She started to walk away.

"Would you stop? Please."

"I have to go to class."

But she stopped. Down the hall, the jock who'd waved was looking at me like, *Why's he talking to her?* But I knew why. Because she'd been my friend when I'd had no others. Because of guilt. So, I said, "Look. We're still friends."

"Were we ever really?"

"Of course we are." Over her shoulder, I saw Charlie. He stood with Amanda Colbert, gesturing at me. I pretended not to see and walked all the way to class with Binky. The next day, I had lunch with her. It was the least I could do.

Friday, after school, I waited until Mom was half-hypnotized by Rosie O'Donnell, so she wasn't watching her purse. It was on the kitchen counter, behind her. I opened the refrigerator, using the door as a shield so she wouldn't see me rifling through it.

"Paul, you drinking soda again?"

Nabbed. "No, I was just . . ." I glanced around, finding something easy. ". . . getting some grapes."

She glanced back at me, and I struggled to make eye contact. Lying to her was easier than I'd thought. I was so tired of being good. Behind the door, my fingers searched. Could she see the movement? No. Found them. My hand closed around them, so they'd make no sound. I shoved her key chain into my pocket.

"Sounds good. I'd like some, too." Her voice reproached me. Normally, I'd have offered. She turned back to Rosie, who was talking to some woman from *Saturday Night Live.*

I fumbled with the purse, almost dropped it, caught it by its strap. I stuck the purse on the counter, then arranged it like it had been in case maybe she'd memorized its position. Not paranoid at all, Charlie would have said.

I found the grapes and washed them, not noticing the water was hot until it burned me, then still letting it run over my hands, long after the grapes were clean. I brought them to her.

She patted the sofa. "Sit with me."

I had no choice, so I sat. I held the bowl in my lap, and we ate grapes for ten mind-numbing minutes. Finally, I stood, holding the grape bowl. "I'll put these in the fridge. I'm going to do homework before dinner."

She seemed satisfied. At least, she kept watching her show.

Then I was working on the key chain. With a knife, I separated the metal rings, switched the keys. The medallion caught my eye. Gate's emblem, a cross. I flipped it over, like Christ wouldn't see if I turned the cross over. But then, I didn't really believe in God anyway. I slipped the key chain back into the purse and rearranged it on the counter.

Charlie answered on the first ring.

"Got it," I said.

"Good man."

"You're sure it will work?"

"Of course it will. You're magic."

CHAPTER SEVENTEEN

Gate at night was a different place. By day, oaks and pines shaded its paths. At night, they blacked the moon, surrounding me like storm troopers. It was black. Hundreds of scurrying feet, none human, filled the parking lot. Fireflies, mosquitoes, nameless night creatures flew in my path. I stepped forward. One step. Two. Getting less cautious. Suddenly, the parking lot was bathed in light. I stopped. Who was there? My head jerked. My pupils dilated. I froze, remembering Dad's long-ago words: *Movement is most of camouflage, Paul. Remember that.*

Bastard. I waited to be caught. Nothing. The lights went out.

I looked up. They blazed on again. I laughed. The floodlights were on a motion sensor. No one there. Still, I flew past the administration building and to the classroom building like something was chasing me.

Charlie was outside. We hadn't taken his car. "Too recognizable," he'd said. Instead, he'd borrowed the housekeeper's Civic. It had been past midnight when we reached the school's iron gates.

"I don't have the gate key," I'd said.

"That's okay. You can squeeze through the hedge."

I could squeeze. And where will *you* be? Charlie was smaller, after all, more able to get between the gate and the hedge-covered chain-link fence. But I hadn't said it. Now, creeping down the cement walkway, into faceless dark, I could be bold and think it. But Charlie had answered my question anyway. As usual, Charlie had all the answers.

"Sorry, Einstein. Can't do it." He rested fingers to brow, tired of the whole thing. "I have a tournament tomorrow."

"What's that got to do with this?"

"Can you see Big Chuck's face if I broke my arm or something squeezing through?" He got a faraway look on his face, like he was actually picturing it. He smiled.

"Charlie?"

The grin vanished. "One time, I got tennis elbow. No practice for weeks. Man, was he mad." He clapped a hand on my shoulder. "Can't have that, can we? Besides, I can barely turn on a computer. I'll be the lookout."

And if I broke *my* arm? Another question I hadn't asked. Hadn't needed to. I knew the answer: He'd drive away.

I understood that. This was *my* job. I was the one

with something to prove.

"Relax, Paul." Again, he'd read my thoughts. "Nothing will happen."

And I'd believed him, sliding between gate and fence, shuffling through dark gravel to the black parking lot with the storm-trooper trees and, now, to Mom's office alone.

Mom worked in the attendance office, in the classroom building. It was breezeway style, open, so I didn't need the key to enter the building, just her office. "No flashlights," Charlie had dictated. "The neighbors might see you. Or Old Carlos." But the janitor's cottage was in back, separated from this building by cities of ficus trees, each with three or four trunks and curtains of hanging moss. A murderer could hide there, unseen. Besides, anyone in his right mind would be asleep now. It was dark, but not as dark as the parking lot. Drops of moonlight seeped through tree limbs like water through a washcloth. I strained to make out room numbers in the dim light. Behind me, footsteps. I turned. Nothing. I fumbled for the key, heard it hit ground and bounce. I searched, sightless, on the ground, finally finding it amid tracked-in gravel and discarded gum. Screw Charlie. Easy for him to say no flashlights. He was in the damn car. I slid the key up to the wall and let it drop into my hand.

No. Charlie was my friend. He wasn't slacking off. He was the lookout. He had to be. And his dad *would* kill him if he hurt himself. Not like me, with no dad to worry about.

Besides, I was part of Charlie's group now, part of his plans. He'd even been taking me with them to lunch. With Amanda, hair like falling leaves. I couldn't think about her now, but I liked to, at strange times of day, or at night, when I squirmed in bed, unable to sleep.

I found the doorknob, inserted the key.

I didn't need lights in the office. Mom's desk was near the window, and the seeping moonlight would illuminate my work. But could you see the monitor's glow through the window? I removed my black Carolina Panthers sweatshirt and hung it so it blocked the light. I threw the switch.

The old system started with a jolt. It ran through its setup, slow. When would it be ready? Finally, a prompt for my name. I typed LAURA. Error. I tried LAURAR. Right.

The password for Mom's computer wasn't hard. "Everyone uses pets' names," I'd told Charlie. That was something I'd learned in chat rooms. I tried it. We'd had a cat, Verdi, in North Carolina.

I typed VERDI.

Access denied.

I tried my own name, first, then middle, then both. Then Mom's maiden name. Finally, I remembered a page from a photo album, a cat my parents had when I was too little even to remember. His name was Macoco, from some old movie.

Macoco was the password.

I needed another password to enter the student-record

databases. A school password. That took longer, running it through different combinations, thanking God or whoever for all the time I'd had on my hands those years, to learn everything computers could do. Finally, I found it. Wait 'til I told Charlie the password was *PiratePrde*. Maybe this wasn't a big deal.

STUDENT NAME: the program prompted.

I hesitated, then typed, CHARLES GOOD JR. Enter.

Charlie's name, address, and reference number flashed on-screen. I exited the window, repeating the number, "1091, 1091, 1091." I typed it in.

Charlie's entire record came up. Near-flawless academics. National Honor Society. Tennis team, captain, honor awards in English, math, social studies, P.E. Perfect attendance six years running. Citizenship award.

The D in biology stuck out among all those A's. I moved Mom's mouse onto it, hit delete, and typed another A, completing the monotonous pattern. Then, I remembered Charlie's caution. "Give me a B. Zaller'd remember an A." I changed it again.

I felt less careful leaving. The deed done, it was simple. Why had I worried? I slammed doors, jumped to hit the red-lit EXIT sign so hard my hand hurt and the sound reverberated through the silent breezeways. I ran through the halls to the parking lot to commune with the moon. I'd done it. I'd cast aside everything Mom or Binky had ever thought about me.

I wasn't a good kid, a good, boring kid. I wasn't some good sucker who'd live slow and die old. I was wild. I was like Dad—Dad who didn't care about, didn't love, anyone.

I scaled the gates this time and free-fell eight feet to the ground like stepping across a mud puddle. Charlie's lights were off. But even in the darkness, I saw him seeing me, seeing me whooping and leaping in the dew-drenched grass. He let me go on. Then, his motor sprang to life. He beckoned to me. I got in, and we roared into the night.

"You did it?" he asked, about a block away.

"You bet, baby!" My voice, my words, like someone else's.

"No one saw?" For once, Charlie looked scared.

"No one to see."

"Maybe this was a bad idea." Charlie's eyes never left the road, but his hands clenched white on the steering wheel. "Maybe we should—"

"Bad idea? Bullshit. You're not going chicken on me now, are you, Charlie?"

"No, it's just . . ." We were blocks away, and Charlie hit his lights. "We may have to do other stuff now, things to cover our tracks."

But I was too euphoric to ask what things. I threw my head back and kicked my legs onto the dashboard. "Whatever it takes, man! Whatever it takes!"

CHAPTER EIGHTEEN

Monday, at school, I waited. For *what*? I didn't know. But that day, I sat in chapel and in class, expecting to hear about the person who'd freaked out their computer system. And when someone from the office came to my class, third period, I figured he was coming for me. It was only a message from some guy's mother. That's when I realized: They weren't coming for me. I'd gotten away with it. Binky had been right. I *was* smarter than they were. It felt good. It felt really good.

Everyone seemed to know I was Charlie's friend now, and that changed everything. When I walked into history, a girl called my name. I recognized her as one of Charlie's group, Kirby, who had blond hair and looked cool even with glasses. A cheerleader. She gestured toward the seat beside her. I sat, cautious, in case she was screwing with me. But no. She leaned on my desk and started describing the concert they'd gone to over the weekend. "You should come with us next time," she said. And later, when Mr. Roundtree had us choose lab partners in chemistry, I didn't have to wait around to see who was left. People wanted me.

I changed in those next weeks. I picked up things from Charlie's crowd. Like St. John's way of walking, thumbs hitched in pockets so his elbows stuck out. And Meat's talk, using words like *gel* and *jacked*, saying *later* instead of *good-bye*.

Now I had lunch at McDonald's with Charlie's group. For months, I'd been less than a peon, pushing a tray in the cafeteria. Now, I'd arrived.

I'd learned to call it Mickey D's as Charlie's friends did. The Monday after Charlie and I broke into school, we arrived at ten after, three carloads, including Amanda, Kirby, and Emily. We took St. John's Bronco, him eyeing Amanda pulling into the space beside us. I tried not to. St. John still liked her, which about killed my chances. Not that I had much chance anyway. Still, I held the swinging door while all three girls stepped through. Charlie, St. John, and Meat walked ahead of me to the counter.

"We'll sit outside," Charlie announced when we'd gotten our trays.

"There's only one table left out there." St. John gestured toward the play area. "And all those kids." He pretended to shudder. I was busy getting ketchup. I pressed the dispenser top, and ketchup dribbled out, like blood from a paper cut.

"Well, I'm sitting outside." Charlie turned. Meat and I followed him.

Outside was crawling with kids, like St. John said. And moms, arms dripping with babies and Happy Meal toys. Ball-pit balls sailed through the air. Kids screeched. One woman breast-fed, hunched over, trying and failing to cover her nipple with her kid's head. Meat gave her a long look until she turned away. The others glared at us. Still, I followed Charlie. When we reached the lone table, one of those round concrete ones I'd only seen in Miami, Charlie sat.

"Sit here, Einstein." Charlie motioned to the seat beside him.

I took it, sliding Big Mac and fries off my tray to take up less room, trying not to grin.

"Now you." With his hand, he beckoned to Amanda, whose auburn hair and plastic-encased salad both shimmered in the noonday sun. "Sit by Paul."

Amanda obeyed, thigh brushing mine on the narrow bench. My hand jerked. Fries skittered across the table. *Be cool.* I stared into white-hot sun, not daring to look at St. John. After all, I was just following orders.

Charlie continued that way. Meat, he assigned the seat on Amanda's other side, then Kirby, Pierre, Emily, and Ryan, squeezing seven onto benches meant for four. When no one else would fit, Charlie smiled. "The rest will have to sit on the ground."

The others shuffled a little but obliged. All but St. John. He glared at Charlie, eyes like cold marbles. Charlie looked back.

"Sorry," Charlie said. "Hadn't realized you were still with us, buddy."

"Maybe I'm not." St. John walked to the overflowing garbage pail, shoved his lunch, tray and all, inside, then stalked from the restaurant. Seconds later, his motor roared.

Then, silence.

Charlie broke it. "Oops." He smiled, like a kid who's spilled milk but knows he won't get in trouble. Everyone laughed.

Amanda tipped her head, eyes meeting mine, then Charlie's. "He can be so . . . you all can squeeze into my car."

That's when I noticed it for the first time. Her retainer. It rested against her top teeth, challenging anyone to think she wasn't perfect. I couldn't speak. Charlie took over. "Great." He blessed Amanda with a smile. "And Paul here will repay the favor. You said you were having trouble in computer-science class."

Amanda's smile vanished. "Wilburn's just waiting to flunk my ass." In her voice, even the word "ass" sounded pretty. "Now why'd you have to go mention that? You spoiled my lunch."

Kirby interrupted. "You never eat, Amanda. Or you puke it out when you do."

"That's a lie." Amanda's green eyes were on me now, pleading. "Paul barely knows us, and now he'll think bad things about me."

My face felt nuked. I wanted to say that was impossible. But I'd lost my ability to speak.

Charlie leaned across me to Amanda, like coconspirators. "The reason I mentioned it is, Paul here is a computer genius. He could help you out. Right, Paul?"

I tried my tongue. Nope, still not working.

"Would you?" Amanda asked.

"Sure," I managed.

She was only agreeing with Charlie, I told myself. I glanced at him, and he smiled back, angelic. I watched Amanda's fingers, sunned and slender, tipped in white with one gold ring. It was a heart.

I opened my bedroom door. Mom stood, holding a sweatshirt. My sweatshirt. The black Carolina Panthers one I'd draped over her computer monitor Saturday night. I must have forgotten it there. *Oh, crap.*

"I found this." She held it with accusing fingers. I didn't meet her eyes. She knew nothing, I reminded myself. The sweatshirt proved nothing. Besides, she wasn't so pristine, wasn't so pure. I'd only thought that because she locked me away from the world and kept me for herself. I made a mental note to tell Charlie about this later. Charlie would be proud I'd figured her out.

"Paul?"

I stared at her, at the sweatshirt until it all blurred together like a Rorschach inkblot. I closed my eyes. They were still there.

I opened my eyes. I said nothing.

"Please answer me." She still held the sweatshirt, face serene, like Binky's weeping Madonna.

I said nothing.

"I don't like this behavior, Paul." Her face crumpling. "Are you . . . on drugs or something? I don't like how these friends have influenced you."

"I bet you don't. You don't want me to have friends." I heard, almost *saw* the words streaming from my mouth. My voice sounded unfamiliar, confident. Charlie's voice.

Mom stood, mouth slightly open. Then she closed it. "Paul, don't be silly. Of course I want you to have friends. I want you to be happy."

"Yeah, you were dying for me to have friends. That's why you kept me locked up all those years like . . . Skinner." Somehow that came to me. We'd read about Skinner, a scientist who tried out his behavioral experiments on his own daughter, keeping her in a box like a rat. That was exactly what my mother had done. Exactly. "You just used me."

My blood was pumping. It felt so good. Why hadn't I known how good it would feel?

I'd thought she'd shut up then, but she didn't. She came closer, still holding the sweatshirt, gesturing with it.

"Don't change the subject, Paul. How did this get there?"

"What do you care?" But thinking, *How much does she know?*

"What do I care? It's my computer, my job. Were you there, Paul?"

"How would I have gotten there?"

"I don't know. You tell me. After school, maybe? Did you sneak in after school Friday and use my computer for something?"

"No."

"To look at porn or something? Or play those awful games?"

"No."

She'd backed me into a corner. I pushed past her, brushing against the sweatshirt, making it drop to the floor. She tried to block my way, but I walked right through her to the door and down the stairs to the parking lot. She followed me to as far as the elevator, but when I yelled, "I can't believe you don't trust me!" she retreated back into the apartment.

I found the pay phone in the parking lot and called Charlie.

CHAPTER NINETEEN

"Why do you hate your dad so much?"

We'd been spending more and more time at Charlie's. Afternoons, we'd do homework in his room, watch the Cartoon Network, or just fool around on his computer. That was what we were doing that day. We'd found some cool websites, tricks to play, like putting sugar in people's gas tanks. Weird satanic stuff Mom would have hated. Even instructions on how to make a bomb. When he didn't answer, I tried again.

"Big Chuck," I said. "Why do you hate him so much?" Even as I said it, part of me couldn't believe I'd asked something so personal. Charlie'd never said he hated his father. But somehow, I knew he did.

Charlie shrugged. He wasn't going to answer. I glanced at the computer screen, trying to find a safer subject. I scrolled through my search result, entered one site, then exited. Charlie drew a long breath. The sound startled me. Then, his voice.

"We were always, like, this perfect family," he said. "Mary quit the fast track a few years to do the PTA crap. Chuck was brownnosing for partnership with this big-deal firm downtown. Every winter, we vacationed in Vail; Carolina mountains every summer. And in between, they were the perfect parents with the perfect kid." He thumbed his chest.

"They had this story they'd tell everyone about my birth. How they'd wanted to fill their empty lives by having a child. But they couldn't. They tried everything, looser-fitting shorts for Big Chuck, special exercises. Nothing. Finally, they gave up and went on a big vacation. They were going to see America. In Washington State, they found God.

"They were north of Seattle, near Skagit, looking for their white-water rafting group. They got off I-5 too soon and couldn't see in the fog. Suddenly, this church just appeared from the mist—nothing else around. Somehow, Mary convinced Big Chuck to ask directions.

"Chuck had on swim trunks and a sweatshirt. Mary pulled some jogging pants over her swimsuit. They were looking for the entrance, when, suddenly, a man came from a hidden doorway. 'Come in, my children,' he said. 'I've been expecting you.'

"Big Chuck tried to explain that they just needed directions.

"'I have the direction you need.' The minister held up his hand, and they followed him into the sanctuary. Chuck was still trying to explain that they only needed to get to I-5. Still, they followed. The church seemed to grow bigger as they walked until it was like St. Patrick's Cathedral out in the boonies."

I watched Charlie. I could barely make out his face in the shadow from the sun. He stared ahead, repeating the tale like it was legend, not just some dumb story his parents told. So I believed it too.

"'You are troubled, my children?' the minister asked. Chuck started to explain again about directions to I-5. But Mary began to cry. In the minister's arms, she repeated the whole story, and as she spoke, light began streaming, red, green, purple, and gold, through the stained-glass windows. The minister said, 'God has heard.'

"He sent them away without directions. But Chuck found I-5 almost immediately, and they made their rafting trip. When they got home, Mary was pregnant. The miracle baby—" Charlie indicated himself —"was born nine months later. Funny thing, when they tried to contact that church to make a donation, there wasn't any such church."

I figured he'd finished his story. It didn't answer my question. Or make sense, for that matter. Still, Charlie seemed to expect a response, so I said, "Weird."

"Not that weird. There's more." Charlie leaned his chair back, getting comfortable, as usual. He didn't look at me.

"My first ten years, I heard that story, like, a hundred times. Every holiday at the club, every family soiree. Chuck and Mary, the perfect parents. And I bought into their crap, so I was perfect too. Perfect grades, perfect at sports. Until sixth grade. It all fell apart. I flunked math. Had to do summer school and couldn't go to this special tennis camp Big Chuck had arranged." He looked out the window. I followed his eyes to the tennis court. "You'd think my perfect father would be a little understanding, but he wasn't. He got so bent up, screaming about school, about me, how stupid I was, screwing up my chances like that. And finally, I yelled back, 'I don't want to play tennis anymore ever! I hate it! I hate you!'

"For weeks, I wouldn't play. Big Chuck tried punishments, bribes, telling me how much fun it was, all the usual parental blackmail. Then, he grabbed my collar and told me I'd play whether I wanted to or not. I ran upstairs, freaked out. He'd never gotten that mad at me before."

I nodded, remembering all the fights Mom and Dad had about me. Charlie continued.

"That night, Mary and Chuck argued. It was the first time I'd ever heard them fight—can you believe that? I tried not to listen. But they were yelling so loud, and at one point, Mary said, 'Give him space, Chuck. He's not you.'"

Charlie stopped, staring at the ceiling. Seconds, almost a minute, passed. I'd never noticed how loud the little fan in the hard drive was. Was he going to finish? Finally, I said, "What did he say?"

"Forget it." Charlie lowered his chair legs, his own legs, to the ground. "Not important. Just sewage under the bridge. Let's do something else." He reached for the mouse.

"Come on, Charlie." I didn't know why it was so important to me that he finished. But it was. "What'd he say?"

Charlie looked at me. "He said, 'I know he's not *me*, Mary. He's not even mine.'"

I squirmed in my seat, then looked away.

"First, I thought it was, like, just something he said," Charlie said. "You know, 'cause he was mad at me. I mean, our lives revolved around each other. He was my *dad*, for Christ's sake. But Mary didn't answer. That freaked me out. She was always talking lawyer talk, about defending yourself, silence as an admission of guilt. But when he said that, she was silent. Finally, she laughs and says, 'So, he screws up, he's my kid?'

"But it was too late. Big Chuck said, 'I know, Mary. I've always known. I can't father children, and I don't believe in miracles. So I had us tested. He's not mine.'"

"Yikes," I said. Meat's word. Charlie nodded.

"I was in the hall by then, listening, ready to leap if the doorknob turned. But it didn't. Mary starts bawling, saying it's not true. But finally, she confesses. It was someone from her office, didn't mean anything. 'Can't you see, Chuck? It was the only way.' But Big Chuck wasn't listening. He was out of there."

"Yikes," I repeated, just because it seemed appropriate. "What happened?"

Charlie looked at me like I was stupid. "You know what happened. We're still here. He came back, of course. But everything had changed. I wasn't a miracle. I wasn't golden."

But you were, I wanted to tell him. *You are.* I didn't say it. It would sound queer.

"And I knew I couldn't screw up again," he continued. "I had to stay . . . perfect or it would all fall apart. He'd stop even pretending to be my dad."

I watched him, understanding. Charlie was like me, a regular person. It made me value him more than ever. And I understood something else.

"So the D in Biology . . . ?"

"I can't get D's," Charlie said. "The ironic thing is, we got closer after that. Mary went back to work that year, so Big Chuck cut his hours to spend time at home, practice with me so I could . . . fulfill his expectations of what his son should be, even though I wasn't."

"That must be rough."

Charlie looked surprised. Then, he shrugged. "Not at all." He reached across me for the mouse. He went to his Favorite Places and chose a site. It connected.

The screen shouted, PYROMANIA!!!

He didn't want to talk anymore, so I gestured toward the screen. "What's that?"

"A bomb website. This one's pretty cool. When I found it last night, I couldn't wait to show you."

"Really?" Though Charlie and I were best friends now, it

was still unbelievable to me that he thought about me when I wasn't there.

"Yeah, I bookmarked it so I'd remember."

I scrolled down, past pictures of buildings exploding, the page lined with smiley faces that looked like they were on acid. The site even had heavy metal playing. The links flew by.

EXPLOSIVES

INCENDIARIES

MOLOTOV COCKTAIL RECIPE 1

MOLOTOV COCKTAIL RECIPE 2

MOLOTOV COCKTAIL RECIPE 3

"What's a Molotov cocktail?" I asked.

"Click on it," Charlie said, grinning.

I did. This was so cool.

Then, hall footsteps. A voice. "Charlie?"

"Yes, sir." Charlie grabbed the mouse from me and, with two hand flicks, exited the window, then the Internet. "Time for practice," he said.

CHAPTER TWENTY

Charlie was my best friend now. And he had all sorts of other friends too. Maybe they wouldn't have accepted me, but with Charlie, they had to. I was always with Charlie. I followed him, went where he went. I finally belonged.

The day after Charlie told me the story about his dad, he pulled me aside in the hall. "What I told you yesterday?"

"Yeah?"

"I never told anyone that. Not Meat or St. John. No one." He flicked a hair from above his eyebrow. "Understand?"

I promised to tell no one. But secretly, I felt like one of the Chosen.

A few days later, Amanda cornered me at Mickey D's.

It was one of those days when everyone from Gate and everyone from Palmetto High had converged on Mickey D's. So, I was assigned to hold a table while Charlie, Meat, and St. John, braving the glares of the Palmetto students, ordered lunch. I was cleaning dried ketchup off the Formica with my jacket sleeve when suddenly, she was there.

"This seat taken?"

I stopped cleaning, let my arm fall to my lap, and glanced around, over her head. Did she mean some other seat, some other guy? Probably just wanted to wait for St. John. It was a booth for four. I looked at Charlie. Across the restaurant, he mouthed something. I think it was, *Go for it, stupid.* He grinned. Amanda was looking down at where my arm had disappeared under the table. I jerked it up, so she wouldn't think I was playing with myself or something.

She slid her tray, slid her body against mine. Too close. No, no such thing. "Okay?"

"Sure. I mean, no." Our thighs touched—an accident. She couldn't possibly have meant it. "I mean, sit down." Though, obviously, she already had.

She laughed. "You're pretty funny."

"Thanks." Trying to think of something to say. Ask her about her computer-science work, maybe. I'd never helped her with that. No, too geeky. She was probably just being nice. Finally, I blurted, "I liked what you read that day in Bundy's class. About how hard it was making friends here."

She looked away. "Oh."

"Sorry." Now she knew I'd been watching her all semester.

"No, I . . . I never told anyone that before. My friends all ragged on me about it."

"They shouldn't have. I knew how you felt."

"But you're different." She looked down, touching but not eating her fries.

"Different?"

"In a good way. Better than them, someone I could really talk to." She looked up then, meeting my eyes. "It's so hard, trying to do what people expect of you."

"Yeah, I know what you mean." I leaned close to her.

"Way to hold a table, Richmond." St. John's voice boomed above everything, even my heartbeat. He threw a bag at me—my lunch. Had he gotten it to go on purpose? The others had trays. Still, I took it.

"Oh, sorry." Amanda moved away. "Paul said it wasn't taken." She started to pull a chair from the next table.

"It isn't," I started to say. But St. John's voice stepped on mine.

"I saw your friends over there, Amanda," he said. "Why don't you leave?"

Charlie and Meat had taken seats across from me, but St. John stood there, holding his tray, blue eyes freezing both of us out. "Why don't you leave?" he repeated. Not to Amanda.

"Sure." Amanda stood. "'Bye, Paul."

And before I could do anything else, she was across the room, laughing with Emily and Kirby.

St. John didn't talk during lunch. Actually, no one said much. I spent the half hour trying to make eye contact with

Amanda. But driving back to school, St. John said, "She doesn't really like you, you know."

We turned past this wayside park. The sun off the water hit my eyes. I squinted. I said the only thing that came to mind. "Really?"

"No, she's just jerking you around to piss me off."

Of course it was true. I'd always known that. Someone like her would never like someone like me. But I was tired of feeling like that. Charlie was in the front seat, and I took my bravery from him. So, I said, "That's funny. I thought she broke up with you."

"Because I found someone better."

"Yeah? Where is she now?"

Charlie leaned back to look at me, then St. John, and said, "Quit it. Both of you."

"Why should I?" St. John accelerated through the turn, and the whole car went sideways. "I'm sick of him. Charlie here wants a fan club instead of friends, so he chooses this loser." He jerked a thumb at me. "And we let him hang with us out of the goodness of our hearts. Hell, I'll say it, out of pity. Pity because his mom's a peon, and he's too stupid to—"

"Shut up!" The words tore from my throat. My arm jerked, reflexive, my hand grabbing his neck without me knowing what I was doing. But it held tight. If I'd had one of Dad's guns, he'd have been dead. My fingers tensed, nails gripping his throat.

St. John shut up. I saw his face in the rearview. Red, freaked out. His eyes, icy the second before, showed something else. Fear. Of me? Me? Behind me, Meat tugged my arm, begging me to stop; the car was moving, for Christ's sake. What was I trying to do? St. John veered left, then right, me still clutching him, wanting to hurt him. But Charlie got the wheel straight and, finally, Meat eased me off St. John's throat. We pulled into school. St. John cut the motor.

"Out!" he said, mostly to Charlie.

"You're acting like a child, Gray," Charlie said.

"I don't want to hear it. I don't want to hear *you.* You're going to have to find someone else to do your shit work from now on."

I didn't know what that meant, didn't even think that much about it. I was still dazed, wondering where it had come from. That anger. That violence in me. And then, the high, better than alcohol, the high of having hurt someone else for once, instead of the other way around.

Lara escaped the burial chamber and was attacked by seven henchmen. The fragmatch was on. Lara fragged them with her Uzi. The last one dropped the Jeep keys. More bots came after her, toting machine guns. She tried the Uzi again. Click. No ammo.

"Uzis really eat ammo," I said.

"Drive over them with the car," Charlie urged.

That worked. I got the keys and advanced to the next level. Then, I saved the game before anything else could attack me.

"You can keep playing," Charlie said.

"Won't your dad be home?" I glanced at the clock.

"Yeah, you're right," Charlie said. He walked to the bed and fell facedown onto it, a dramatic move, showing his boredom with everyone and everything. He lay there, ten seconds, twenty seconds. More. Just when I thought he was napping, his voice came, muffled by the mattress. "Could you ever really kill someone?"

I must have heard him wrong. "What?"

He lifted his head just enough so I could see brown eyes looking at me from under his hair. "Do you ever wonder how it would feel to kill someone for real?"

Yes, my mind screamed before I could stop it. When everyone at school was picking on me, picking on me, picking on me. Or St. John, the other day. Even Mom sometimes. The idea of vaporizing them. Imagine the power. The power. But I shook my head. "You crazy?"

Charlie sat up and laughed. "Don't you know when I'm screwing with you, Einstein?"

I laughed too. "Sure."

CHAPTER TWENTY-ONE

The next day, I saw Binky again in the hall. Though we had three classes together, we'd been talking less and less. That day, though, I found her before school. She sat on a bench, reading.

I stood beside her, waiting. I couldn't say why. Maybe guilt. When she didn't look up, I said, "Hi."

She still didn't look up. I was thinking about walking away, but I didn't. Binky finished the page, turned the next one, then marked it with her silver bookmark. She stood. "Richmond, do you ever wonder why, when birds fly in formation, one side's always longer than the other?"

I played along. "Why?"

She smiled. "Because one side has more birds on it."

"What's that supposed to mean?"

"It means, sometimes something's really obvious, Richmond—if you think about it."

"Like what?" Though I knew she was talking about Charlie. Charlie and me. She was jealous, of course.

"He's using you."

"For what?"

She wavered. "I don't know yet, but he is."

"So you're saying no one could be friends with me without some sort of . . . ulterior motive."

"I didn't say that. I was friends with you." I noticed the word *was*.

"Then what?" I demanded.

"Charlie Good doesn't operate like that. He doesn't have friends, he has . . ." She looked down at her book but, finding it closed, she stood. "Just think about it."

"About what?"

"This . . . this . . . hold he has over you. I see you in the halls with him, following him like the guy at the circus who sweeps up after the elephant. What is it?"

"Nothing. He doesn't have a hold over me. We're friends. Just friends."

But I knew what she meant, and it wasn't true. It wasn't that. Somehow, I had to prove that to her. So, I leaned over, right there in the hall, caressed her coarse, rough hair, then pulled her toward me in a clumsy kiss—my first. I didn't really know how to do it, so I held her close, willing myself to be into her, be attracted to her. And I tried not to admit that it was because of Charlie, because I was so out of my league with his group. No. I just felt bad about Binky. She'd been my friend, after all, when no one else had. I kissed her again.

She pushed me away. For a second, I thought she'd slap me, spit at me. Punch me, even. I'd have deserved it. But instead, she looked about to cry. She started to walk away, then turned back and gathered herself so she could speak.

"I thought you were different," she said. "But you aren't. You think you can use people's feelings against them. You're exactly like the rest of them—you belong together."

"But—

"Go to hell."

I started to protest, but she hit me with a look that hurt and was gone. I knew we wouldn't speak again. I'd lost her. Now, I only had Charlie.

The next day, I found a paper stuck through the slats of my locker. A note.

Ask Charlie who killed the dog.

I crumpled it. I figured I knew who'd sent it.

Charlie and Meat picked me up Friday night. "Mr. St. John is no longer part of our set," Charlie said with no trace of regret. Sometimes, he sounded like rich guys in cartoons. We took Meat's car to Sunset Place, an outdoor mall near school, and I watched Charlie and Meat try to pick up these dark-haired twins outside Bath & Body Works. Meat even went inside and let one girl spray stuff all over him.

Then, their parents showed up.

"Shoot." Meat displayed his body-glitter-covered biceps. "I smell like watermelons, and I didn't even score a phone number."

"No love tonight," Charlie said, laughing. "That cat marked her territory."

A reggae band was playing on the second-floor landing, and Meat bobbed to the music. I tried to, but I always felt like a dork, dancing. We hung over the railing a while and watched the girls go by. Charlie said, "How goes it with Mandy?"

"It's not going."

"Why? You're not into her?"

"It's not that. That would be impossible. She's sort of . . . out of my league."

Charlie's eyes followed a girl below, a blonde whose tank top gave an almost unobstructed view of her breasts. I wondered if I'd ever touch a girl's breast. But he said, "You're in the big leagues now, Paul. No girl's out of reach."

I shrugged. "Maybe you're right."

"Of course I am."

Meat interrupted. "But me—I've got no chance with this glittery watermelon crap on."

We laughed. It was after eleven by then, so we decided to leave. It was raining, and the road shone. We passed a massive

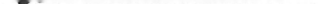

church, then stopped for a light. The red glowed off the slick pavement. Charlie gestured toward the roadside.

"Some girl bought it here," he said. "Where that ficus is. She was skating on the bike path and got nailed by a car. Died on impact."

"I remember that," Meat said. "Girl from Sacred Heart was driving with her friends. She had, like, ten shots of vodka and a joint, and it was still broad daylight. They say the skater saw the car coming, but there was nowhere to hide."

The light changed, but we stayed there. We watched the ficus tree turn green in the reflected light. When Meat pulled out, he drove slower.

Charlie said, "And the moral of this story, children, is: Don't get caught."

Meat laughed, but I didn't. I looked back at the tree until long after we'd disappeared around the curve. I couldn't tell whom Charlie had meant. The driver? Or the skater?

We drove in silence. Finally, Charlie said, "The Mailbox Club is dead, men. We need new material." When no one responded, Charlie turned to me. "Any ideas, Einstein? Got to start contributing sometime."

I didn't answer. We were near Binky's house. And her church. The perfect place for Charlie to trash—with the open door, we wouldn't even have to break in. But when I started to say it, my mouth wouldn't move. I remembered my wish that night. God. It had come true.

"I've got *nada*," I said. "Sorry."

Charlie gazed at me a second, like he knew there was something I wasn't telling. Then, he smiled. "It's okay, Paul. I know I'll get some return on my investment in you someday."

And since he was smiling, I smiled too. At least that meant he planned to keep me around.

That night, lying in bed, I thought about the note I'd gotten about Trouble. Thing was, I'd seen Binky's handwriting before. The handwriting on the note wasn't Binky's. But it had to be Binky who sent the note. Everyone else loved Charlie.

CHAPTER TWENTY-TWO

I never truly felt comfortable with Charlie's friends. What St. John said was probably true—the people who were my friends were the same people who'd hated me before. They only tolerated me because of Charlie. So I was surprised, on the way home from school the next week, when Charlie said, "Party at Pierre's Friday. On the beach."

"So?" I felt a twinge in my stomach.

"So, you're going, right?"

"No. He didn't invite me."

"*I'm* inviting you. Same thing."

"But it's his party."

"So what? He's going to swoop down and throw you out?" Charlie laughed. "*I* want you there. Everyone else respects what I want."

I chewed on that a minute, watching Charlie's hands on the leather steering wheel. It was flattering, him wanting me there so much. Of course, I wanted to go. And Charlie was right. I was safe with him.

"Besides," he said, "Amanda will be there."

He smiled, watching my reaction. I shook my head. But I knew I was going. Charlie always knew just what to say to convince me.

"I can't stay too late," I told Charlie at lunch the day of the party. "My mom . . . she's weird about stuff like that."

An exaggerated sigh from Charlie. "Can't spell *smother* . . ."

"Yeah, yeah, without *mother*."

Later, Charlie suggested I stay over his house that night. That way, my mother wouldn't know how late I stayed out. "And what Mama doesn't know won't hurt her," Charlie said.

It sounded like a great idea. To cement the deal, I approached Mom in the attendance office with the news. "Catch them off guard," Charlie had said. "Don't give them time to think of reasons to say no."

I chose the passing period between fifth and sixth. Four minutes. One of the other secretaries stood at Mom's desk when I entered. I pushed through the swinging half-door to where Mom sat.

"Hey."

I'd barely spoken to her since the day with the sweatshirt. But I gave her a kiss on the cheek before starting. That was Charlie's suggestion. Then, I started in.

"It's okay if I stay over at Charlie's tonight, right?" *Always phrase the question to suggest a "yes" answer,* Charlie had said.

Mom looked up, then down, distracted. "Paul, you remember Mrs. Vega, don't you?"

I put out my hand, did the polite-boy thing.

"Charlie's house?" I said.

She pulled a hair. "I don't know."

"Charlie Good?" Mrs. Vega piped in, her face going all warm and fuzzy. "Are you friends with Charlie?" Then, to Mom, "Laura, Charlie Good is a sweet boy. A straight-A student. He helped us rearrange the file system last year—on a Saturday." She looked up at me again, like she hadn't really noticed me before. "You're friends with Charlie?"

I nodded, wondering if helping in the office was how Charlie knew so much about everyone. Mrs. Vega and I both looked at Mom, awaiting her response.

"Well . . . I suppose I can't forbid it."

"Great. I'll go home with him, then." I leaned to give her another cheek kiss, pumped Mrs. Vega's arm again, and I was gone.

But when I got to the party, I sort of wished Mom had forbidden me. The day had been fun up to then. We'd gone to the beach, then to Meat's house for dinner. But when we got to Pierre's house, everything changed.

It wasn't the house—though that was part of it. Pierre

lived on Key Biscayne, this island connected by a bridge to downtown Miami. "Where the rich people live," Meat said in the car.

They were all rich to me, so I kept quiet.

The house was about the size of our whole building. We were late. Still, Charlie managed to maneuver his car into the last close parking space. He pushed open the front door, and we followed through the scattered beer bottles and the stench of beer and what I figured was grass.

"You said his parents were home," I said.

"Why would anyone have a party when his parents are home?" Charlie said. Then, "Relax, Einstein. I'll get you home safe to Mommy."

I started to protest, but he motioned us onto the patio, where Meat immediately joined a clump of jocks swapping sports stories in the corner. I followed Charlie. He fished two beers from a cooler and handed me one. "You need it," he said.

I started to open it. The rough metal top bit my hand. I tried not to show it, but Charlie saw. He took the bottle, popped it open against the counter—which was some kind of rock—then, his own. He handed mine back.

I drank it fast. Charlie held his, not drinking. He eyed a group of cheerleaders, juniors I didn't know. They all wore thong bikinis, and one blonde looked back at Charlie. She waved.

Charlie laughed. "Need me to open one of those for you too?"

I laughed too long, felt sick. I downed the rest of the beer, and Charlie handed me his untouched one.

"You okay awhile?" he said.

No, I wanted to say. *Are you kidding?*

But I said, "Sure," and he walked off to join Meat and his friends by the Jacuzzi.

I went the other way. Out of the corner of my eye, I saw Amanda. She wore a red tank suit, the kind swimmers wore, and her hips gyrated to music from inside the house. I thought she saw me. She didn't smile or wave, though. I walked closer, past the pool, to the patio railing overlooking the beach. When I passed her, I said, "Hey."

"Hey." She turned back to Kirby.

Down below, the waves broke, white foam against black. Could I go back to where Amanda stood? No way. I twisted my head, searching for Charlie. Nowhere. I edged closer to Amanda's group and stood on the perimeter a second. When she still didn't turn, I moved on, to the coral steps that led down to the beach. I watched the white foam again for what seemed like hours. Where was Charlie? Why was I even there?

"Hey."

I turned.

The girl was pretty, with long, dark hair and a tiny bikini. I'd seen her around school, but we'd never spoken. She wasn't part of Charlie's group. A butterfly tattoo spread its wings between her breasts.

"Hello?" she said.

I realized I'd been looking at her breasts. I forced my eyes up. "Hey."

"Want to dance?"

"No one's dancing."

"So? There's music. We'll start something."

She took my arm and led me closer to the steps. Her body locked onto mine. She was tall too, and her long, bare legs brushed mine, hips close, leaving me breathless. She smelled of the beach. She swayed to the music's beat. My left hand stole down her back. The other hand was trapped between us, close, so close to her breast. My knuckles brushed the outline of the tattoo. It was a fake. Why was she dancing with me? I felt so buzzed, not just from the beers, but from the music and the surf, the heat of her.

"What's your name?" I asked finally.

"Caroline." She leaned closer, breasts pressing into my hand. Oh, God.

"I'm Paul."

"I know."

The song ended, and she pulled from me. "Gotta go. Thanks for the dance, Paul."

"But—"

But she was gone, faster than she'd been there, running

down to her group of friends. I began to follow. When I reached the top of the stairs, I heard her say, "Did it." She laughed and pretended to brush herself off. "Not that bad. He only drooled a little. Your turn, Courtney. Truth? Or dare?"

"I'll take truth. Can't handle that kind of dare."

My fist clenched around the handrail, the beach swimming below. Their shrieks of laughter burned in my ears. I turned and went into the house.

I had to find Charlie. It was his fault I was there, so he had to take me home. In the living room, I looked left, then right. Finally, I saw him on the stairway. With a girl. The cheerleader who'd waved at him, Lauren, the tiny one who topped the pyramids. They kissed. She laughed and untucked Charlie's white tank top, letting her hands slide across his chest. Charlie kissed her again, led her upstairs. I went for another beer.

This time, I chose a can, reaching through the ice and water and slush until my hands hurt from the cold. I found a lounge chair in the dark near the wall and settled down to drink it. I hated being there. I hated Gate. I hated them all, even Charlie. I thought of the note, *Ask Charlie* . . . But that was just Binky, being jealous. I lay back. My feet felt heavy. I tried to will myself to get up for another beer.

"Hi, Paul."

In the dim light, her face took a second to register. Just a second. It was Amanda.

"Want to walk on the beach?" she said.

"Is this a dare?" Instantly, I was sorry I'd asked.

"What?"

"Nothing." I pretended to take a sip from the empty can, then crumpled it.

"So, do you?"

She was so pretty, even in the dark. She held out her hand. I took it, stood. Then, we were across the patio, going down past the laughing group and Caroline. House music faded. Surf music took over. Our feet hit sand, and she removed her sandals, so I took off my own shoes too. I gripped Amanda's fingers. Was I hurting her? I loosened up. She laughed and pulled me a few steps down the sand.

"Saw you dancing with Caroline Rodgers before."

"Oh."

"She's a bitch."

"Yeah." I swung her arm, watching her hand travel up, past my face, then tried to step closer without her noticing. Impossible. "Thought you weren't talking to me. I mean, you didn't say hello before."

She moved closer. Then, closer still, until there was no blackness between us. She reached up, arm circling my shoulders, my neck, her tongue, somehow, part of my head. For an instant, I tried to stay back, not let her feel my hard-on against her. But only for an instant. Then, her mouth pressed in, and I forgot about Caroline and Charlie, Binky, Mom, and everything, everything but Amanda's mouth, her body on mine.

When we finally separated, she said, "Still worried about whether I said hello?"

I started to say no, but she kissed me again. I crushed in toward her. We sunk down, down into the black sand. My body felt about to explode. Surf pounded my ears, sand like ice against my heat. My hands knew what to do, and I was on her, on her. And there was nothing else.

"Amanda?"

I could have ignored the voice forever, but Amanda stiffened.

"I hate to interrupt."

Then don't. I couldn't stop my hands, fumbling with Amanda's bathing suit. But Amanda sat up, pushing me up with her. It was Kirby.

She repeated, "I hate to interrupt." Her voice making it clear she didn't care. "But it's past midnight."

"So?"

"So, you know my parents get home at one."

"Shit." Amanda stood, brushing sand from her legs and butt. She turned to me. "Kirby was a ba-a-ad girl. She's grounded, but we snuck out while her parents were at the club." She started toward the stairs, Kirby following.

"Wait!" When they turned, I said, "Can I call you?" I couldn't believe she was leaving.

"I'll see you in school." Amanda ran to the stairs and practically jumped over the group sitting there. I watched her. When my eyes reached the top step, they met St. John's.

Somehow, I knew he'd been watching the whole time. Had the whole thing been to make him jealous?

That night, lying in my sleeping bag in Charlie's room, I felt Amanda, like she was still beneath me. Charlie's voice came from the darkness above.

"Have a good time?" I could hear his grin.

"It was okay."

"Okay? Heard you were rounding third with Colbert on the sand."

I didn't correct him. "Don't know. I think she's just using me to make St. John jealous."

"So?" Charlie laughed. "You need to learn, Paul. Life's on the barter system. We all use one other. It's just a matter of getting something you want in return."

"Right," I said.

Just before I fell asleep, I wondered what Charlie wanted from *me*.

CHAPTER TWENTY-THREE

"Hello."

I hadn't thought about David much since I'd become friends with Charlie. But the Monday after Pierre's party, I saw him again.

It was my own fault. I mean, I could have avoided him. He was in his usual spot, near the bell tower where I used to see him with Trouble. Charlie had a tennis match that afternoon, and, stuck waiting for my mother to drive me home, I'd decided to walk around campus. Now, I saw that my old tree stump was occupied. David sat on it, reading a book.

He'd lost weight since I'd last bothered to look at him. And gained acne. His skin was pale, almost translucent, like David was not of this world. Like a messenger from the hereafter.

"What are you staring at?" he said.

"Nothing." I turned my gaze away. "What are you reading?"

He looked at me a second. Then, instead of handing me the book or just telling me what it was like a normal person, he read:

It was not death, for I stood up

It was not death, for I stood up,
And all the dead lie down.
It was not night, for all the bells
Put out their tongues for noon.

It was not frost, for on my flesh
I felt siroccos crawl,
Nor fire, for my marble feet
Could keep a chancel cool.

And yet it tasted like them all,
The figures I have seen
Set orderly for burial
Reminded me of mine,

As if my life were shaven
And fitted to a frame
And could not breathe without a key,
And 'twas like midnight, some.

When everything that ticked had stopped
And space stares all around,
Or grisly frosts, first autumn morns,
Repeal the beating ground;

But must like chaos, stopless, cool,
Without a chance, or spar,
Or even a report of land
To justify despair.

"Pretty," I said, when he stopped reading and looked at me like he expected a response.

But as the word left my lips, I knew it was the wrong one. The poem was disturbing.

"You think so?" he said, like he knew I didn't. "Emily Dickinson. Ever feel that way?"

"No," I said. But sometimes I did, didn't I? "Do you?"

"Yeah." He stared at the poem a long time, like he was reading it again. "We used to live in Georgia, near my mother's people. It wasn't perfect. We were always poor. But, at least, there were others there like us. Then, my uncle told my father about a job here in Miami. 'A prep school,' he said. 'Where David would have the finest education—to make something of himself.' So, we left there and came here."

"That sucks." Thinking of all the times we'd been uprooted for Dad's career.

"Yeah, I've tried to talk them into letting me move back, live with my grandparents. But they won't."

There was a long silence. I thought of the poem again: *to justify despair.*

"Why don't you . . . ?" I stopped, looking for the right word, the right way to put it. "Couldn't you try to act . . . normal?"

"You mean act like them?" he said, and behind him, I heard the cheerleaders spelling something. I think it was *K - I - L - L !*

"Well . . . yeah." Except I'd wanted to say it some other way. "I mean, so they'd leave you alone."

"Nope." But he looked like he wanted to say something else.

"Why not?"

"I tried that. It didn't help. The price was too high."

"But they'll just keep picking on you."

"It won't be much longer," he said. The cheerleaders had finished their cheer, and I just heard David. "Not much longer."

And suddenly, I couldn't handle being around him anymore. Not for a second. I looked at my watch. Four o'clock. "I have to go," I said. He nodded and went back to his book.

But walking back to find Mom, I kept hearing David's words in my ears: *It won't be much longer.*

Tuesday, it rained all day. Hurricane season was supposed to be over, but this storm was trying to jumpstart it. All gray

morning, rain pounded the classroom doors. Old Carlos scrambled around, putting towels under cracks, and someone started a rumor that we'd get to leave early. Someone else picked up on it, and by third period, it was all over school. Between classes, we ran from one room to another because the rain pushed under the breezeway roofs, misting everything in sight.

Our group was one of the few who left for lunch. "You think we should?" Meat said, staring out at the parking lot deluge. But Charlie said he'd rather get wet than eat cafeteria swill, and of course, I agreed. I always agreed with Charlie.

But on the way back, the rain strengthened. The road was flooded, and our invading tires sent fountains of water back to the clouds. The car ahead was license plate deep.

"We shouldn't have gone," Meat moaned. "We're gonna be late. I've got a quiz in Sheridan."

"You wanted to go too," Charlie snapped.

"I didn't." Meat looked at Charlie, then the rain. "Forget it."

We plowed through another puddle. A child's plastic basketball hoop floated by.

"We should stop," I said suddenly.

"Stop?" Meat stared like I was nuts.

"Yeah. Pull over. We're already late, already in trouble." I had a hiccuppy feeling, like when we went out nights. "Just not go back."

"And do what?" But Charlie stopped the car, turned to me.

"Just not go back. Stay here. Go swimming." I pulled my polo over my head and kicked off my shoes. Before anyone could speak, I shoved open the door. The water and wind pushed against it, but I slid by.

"Hey!" Meat yelled. "What are you—?" I slammed the door. Charlie pulled over in an arc of puddle water. I lunged through it, a wet wall slamming my hair and face. It felt good. I ran, blinking, to meet them. Charlie put the window halfway down and stared at me.

For a minute, I stood, dripping, caught in passing cars' headlights, Charlie's incredulous eyes. What was he thinking? Was I nuts? Too immature? But I crossed my eyes at him, and he grinned.

"Tell them the car stalled out," I yelled.

In the backseat, Meat was still urging Charlie to go, leave without me. Charlie said, "You're crazy, Richmond." And I knew I looked it, water dripping off my hair into my eyes. "And you look like a drowned giraffe."

But he was laughing, peeling off his shirt. He lit from the car with a whoop, his legs meeting knee-deep water. He grabbed my arm, and we stumbled to the roadside, through the spattering, dancing rain. Meat joined us seconds later. We found high ground and jumped up and down, begging cars to splash us. Most obeyed, sending torrents, monsoons over our heads and down. The water knocked us back, hard. We surged forward again, again, wiping rain from our eyes, spitting liquid from laughing lips. It was a baptism. A new life where I had all the fun, the laughter, all the friends I'd ever wanted.

"What if someone sees us?" Meat yelled after a bus's wake knocked us to the ground. "Someone from school?"

"Who cares?" Charlie and I shouted in unison. Another wave swamped us. We fought up, laughing. Meat laughed too. It was okay.

We stayed there over an hour, then drove to Meat's house because he lived closest and his mom was home. We told her the car had stalled, and she served us cocoa and sympathy and provided extra pairs of Meat's enormous pants for Charlie and me to wear while ours tumbled in the kitchen clothes dryer. I even called Mom to let her know where I was. Near dinnertime, Charlie drove me home.

"Pretty wild today, Einstein," Charlie said, pulling into a visitor's spot at our building. I'd long since stopped being ashamed of our apartment. Sure, Charlie had never come upstairs, but it didn't matter to him that I lived there.

"You may be ready for some serious fun," he continued.

I didn't have time to ask what he meant. Mom, who'd probably been watching from upstairs, waded down with her red-and-white striped golf umbrella. "Better go," Charlie said, laughing. "Wouldn't want to get wet."

But the next afternoon, when we were alone in

Charlie's room fooling around on his computer, Charlie turned to me.

"We may need to plant a bomb in Old Lady Zaller's classroom."

CHAPTER TWENTY-FOUR

"What?" I stared at Charlie across the monitor. Outside, a Weed Eater buzzed. Charlie smiled, and I laughed. "You really had me going there, man."

"I'm completely serious." Still smiling. "We've done the research, got the info." He took a disc from the holder and inserted it into the drive. Pressed a button. The hard drive swallowed it like a snake on a mouse. A few clicks of Charlie's fingers. The file opened, screaming purple and orange letters.

TEEN ANARCHY!!!

"Charlie . . ."

But he was scrolling, face still frozen in a half-smile. My eyes shifted back to the screen.

We are teens sick of adults screwing with our world! If we want change, we need to change it even if it means blowing every school away!

Purple skulls and distorted smiley faces framed the text. I

knew the page. We'd found it weeks ago, the day Charlie told me about his father. We'd visited it dozens of times, down-loading recipes for all sorts of explosives, fantasizing about how it would be to blow the school sky-high. But that was what it was, fantasizing. At least for me. I hadn't thought Charlie was serious.

Charlie was still scrolling.

Incendiaries. Fun ways to piss people off with fire.

Scrolling . . .

Needless to say, this information is "for educational pur-poses only." But if you want to use it some other way, what can I do? I mean, who am I, your mother?

Underneath, set off by more skulls, were instructions for a bomb. A bomb that went into a school light fixture.

A bomb.

The Weed Eater went dead. The room was silent, except for the hum of the hard drive. And Charlie's breathing, soft, beside me.

I touched his shoulder. "You crazy, man?" I tried to meet his eyes.

He turned, met mine easily. "Who? Me?" He grinned.

"It's not funny, Charlie." I wanted to shake him but, of course, I didn't. "It's not funny."

"Then go home, Paul. Why not go home to Mother?" He turned away.

I stood, walked around to him, needing to explain. "It's a

bomb, a f—" Maybe I should go. "I never thought you were violent."

"That's what you're worried about?" He eased his chair back. I smelled grass through the open window. "You know me all this time, better than anyone, and you think I want to hurt people? Me? I could never hurt anyone. I'm a total pacifist, Paul."

I looked in his eyes. It seemed impossible. I turned away, shaking my head. "Then why are you saying all this shit?"

"I thought you understood, Paul. Shit. I thought you were my friend, the one person who really knew me." He stopped.

The Weed Eater resumed. I didn't want to leave. I wanted to be okay with him, okay like it was before he'd opened his mouth two minutes before. "But a bomb, Charlie . . ." I could barely say the word. "It's serious."

"I know it is." Charlie's eyes reproached me. "No one would have to get hurt. There are lots of ways we could do this so no one would have to get hurt."

"But someone might."

"No. You've seen the website. We can do stuff with fuses, with time-delay so no one is even there when it goes off." He met my eyes. "Don't you trust me, Paul?"

"Of course I do," I said, way too quickly. But I wanted to agree with him. He'd done so much for me. He'd practically saved my life. "I don't know, Charlie. I mean, it says . . ." The phrase *blowing every school away* jumped out at me. This was real. No way could Charlie talk me out of my knowing that.

"We could rig it to go off while everyone is at chapel," he said. So I knew he'd thought this out. "It'll start a fire, that's all. A harmless little fire where everyone will have fun in the sprinklers." Charlie clicked *Exit*. "A harmless fire that might, incidentally, destroy poor Mrs. Zaller's file cabinet."

Oh, that was it. He was still worried about the D. And his father. He'd mentioned it before, the trouble we'd be in if anyone noticed the grade change. And what would Big Chuck do if he knew about the D? It was too scary to consider. The cabinet held Zaller's hard files with all Charlie's test grades. With that gone, no one would ever find out.

Still, I said, "I don't know, Charlie. I mean, someone could still get hurt in a fire. It would scare the crap out of them, at least."

But the thought hit me. So what? *So what?* They were a bunch of spoiled brats who'd never paid for anything. Maybe they deserved to pay. Or, at least, to get scared shitless. I thought about everything they'd done, everything that had happened to me.

Until Charlie. My loyalty was to Charlie. How could I let him down?

Ask Charlie who killed the dog. Why had his request made me think of the note again?

I put the thought from my mind. It was crazy, thinking like that. "I don't think so. Maybe we can think of some other way to get rid of the test papers."

"No problem." Charlie took the disc from the hard drive, flipping it into his hand. "But think about it. You have time." He reached for his backpack and buried the disc deep inside. "It would be fun, though, wouldn't it?"

I nodded, imagining it, imagining all of them, scurrying like ants. It made me smile. "Yeah, it would be."

That week in chapel, the sermon was "The Terror of Temptations." I squirmed in my seat and tried not to listen. Why did I even care?

CHAPTER TWENTY-FIVE

"I want you to stop seeing that boy."

Mom stood between me and the television. I'd just been flipping through the channels. But now, I bobbed and wove to see it, avoiding Mom's eyes. I didn't answer.

I hadn't gone to Charlie's after school that day. He had practice. At least, that's what he'd said, though his practices seldom ran that late. I tried not to consider the other possibility, that he was so angry I'd refused to plant the bomb, that he didn't want to be friends anymore. He'd said that wasn't it. "Relax, Einie, I have practice. Duty calls." And no one picked on me at school, so it was probably true.

Now, Mom snapped off the televison. "Did you hear me?"

"Yes." Between my teeth.

"Good, then we're agreed." She turned the television back on, started to walk away.

"You have to be nuts if you think I'm listening to you."

She turned back and stood there a moment. I watched her. She was imploding. Silently. Trying to decide whether to scream or cry, which type of emotional blackmail to use. She chose her weapon.

She yanked a hair.

"Quit it," I snapped. I wanted to pull every hair from her head. I grabbed the remote and turned the sound louder. The room filled with the sounds of World Wrestling Federation.

"Why are you behaving like this?" she shrieked over the noise. She walked to the edge of the room, pivoted, and turned back. "Since you've met him, you barely spend an hour at home. You won't talk to me. You're only home for dinner and bed." She sank onto the sofa. "We used to mean so much to each other."

"I never meant anything to you. Not really. Not as your son. As your servant, maybe, or some kind of surrogate husband you didn't have to f— sleep with. Why don't you get a boyfriend? Or any friend and get the hell out of my life!"

I stopped. The words hung there.

"How dare you . . . ?" She was crying now, burying head in hands. The old Paul would have held her, comforted her. This Paul didn't care. "I love you," she sobbed. "I gave up everything for you. Everything."

"What did you give up?"

"You may as well know, I suppose. When your father and I divided our property in the divorce, I told him he could have everything as long as he didn't contest my custody of you."

She looked up at me, triumphant.

I stepped back. "Dad wanted custody?"

"Oh, he said he did." She stopped, stifling leftover sobs with her palm. "He said lots of things, but it was all about money, all about trying to work a good settlement. A good deal. He never loved you like I did."

The meaning soaked in. "So, you *bought* me from him."

"Don't say that. He sold more than I bought. He had a million reasons why I shouldn't have you." She laughed, a high cough. "But the second I said I'd forget the money, I became the perfect mother in his eyes. He told the judge so. So, we agreed. I'd come here with barely a penny to my name. And he'd leave us alone, no matter what."

She kept talking, saying other things, but I wasn't listening. I felt dizzy, sick. All those calls. All those soul-killing calls to my father. He hadn't answered because he loved money. Loved money enough to shut me out forever. And worse. Dad had known all along what a leech Mom was, yet he'd abandoned me to her. And Mom gloried in it. I buried my head in my hands and sat there, willing her to disappear.

The next best thing. The phone rang. I reached for it.

"Don't get that," Mom snapped. She lunged for the end table, but I was faster.

It paid off. It was Charlie.

"Hey, Einstein. How's it going?"

I couldn't even say *fine*.

"Got out early. Come downstairs. I'll swing by and pick you up."

"Sure," I managed. But every bone in my body was thanking God or whoever for Charlie Good.

"I'm going to Charlie's," I said as I hung up. Then, I walked out and downstairs, not even listening to Mom's whining.

"I got your note."

I'd been avoiding Binky. For obvious reasons. But the day after I finally had it out with Mom, I was still feeling defiant. That's why I got to Spanish class early, to talk to Binky.

"What note?" she said. "I didn't write you a note."

"Yeah, right. The note you sent . . . about Charlie. I got it the day after I . . ." I stopped, not wanting to say *kissed you*.

She said nothing for another minute. And in her silence, I realized she was telling the truth. She hadn't sent the note. But who else would imply such a terrible thing about Charlie? I'd been trying not to think about it. But since Charlie had asked me to plant the bomb, it had suddenly become important. If the person who'd written the note really knew something about Charlie, if Charlie had anything to do with what had happened to Trouble, it made the whole thing a lot more serious. Not that I believed that Charlie would do something like that.

Finally, Binky said, "Don't flatter yourself, Richmond. I wouldn't warn you if there was a bear behind you, licking its chops . . . and that's not so far from the truth."

I said, "Charlie's my friend, my real friend."

She nodded. "I hope you're right, Paul."

I had to get out of there. I grabbed my books. There were ten minutes left of lunch hour, so I looked for Amanda. Sometimes, we hung out before class. We hadn't made out again since Pierre's party the week before. Still, I had hopes. But when I found her, she was by her locker, with St. John. He brushed a lock of hair from her eyes. I ducked into the boys' room.

All day long, it bugged me. Who'd sent the note? Then, it hit me.

After class, I didn't wait for Charlie or Mom.

I had to find David Blanco.

CHAPTER TWENTY-SIX

Looking for David felt like a betrayal of Charlie. It meant I believed what the note said—that Charlie had something to do with killing Trouble. But I didn't.

I had no reason to. Charlie had been the best. He hadn't pressured me about setting the bomb. Really, he couldn't have been nicer about it. "I understand," he'd said when I apologized again and again. "You'd do it if you could. You're just scared. Don't worry—we're still friends."

Yet, I was looking for David, going first to the janitor's cottage, tapping on the window I'd figured was his. Then, on the green plywood door. No answer. When I turned to leave, the door squeaked open.

David's mother filled the door frame. I stood a second, awkward, because I'd bought lunch from her a couple dozen times without making eye contact. Now, I did. Maybe I stared. Her obesity was fascinating in its detail, four or five chins, fat even under her eyes. "Is David here? I'm Paul. Paul Richmond."

Slowly, she smiled. "Paul. David's mentioned you." Her English was edged with a southern lilt. "Come in."

"Is he here?"

She shook her head, chins following. "He'd be around somewhere. You'll look for him, honey?"

"I will." I left, feeling her eyes follow me as I walked away.

David could have been anywhere, but I started looking at the back of campus. By the clock tower because that's where I'd always seen him with Trouble. I drifted toward it, still asking myself why I was looking for him.

The clock rang three forty-five. Half an hour, still, until my ride home. I'd made up an excuse not to leave with Charlie that day, told him I was going shopping with Mom, wondering if he knew I was lying. Now, I circled the clock tower, waiting for David to materialize.

A shout pierced the stillness.

"Get away from me, assholes!"

It was David's voice. It came from above and was followed by a scream. My shoulder hit the tower's door, my foot met the lowest stair. I ran up the dim, narrow passage, barely feeling my step's momentum. I reached the top, winded from a run I didn't recall making.

Three people were inside. Two were guys I'd seen at assemblies. They wore Gate's familiar blue student council caps and stood on the gray cement floor inside. The third barely balanced on the narrow gold ledge outside. He held the wall between them. I stared.

He looked unreal, green curls glowing in the dying sun. It was David. On the ledge was David Blanco.

I remembered him reading, *to justify despair.* And I knew. I knew what it was to have more than you could take. But for Charlie, I'd have been there myself. I stepped toward David.

"Stay back!" Then, his face changed. He recognized me. He raised one hand, holding tight with the other. The two guys rushed toward him. Again, he shrieked, "Stay back!"

They backed off. David stared.

"Get out," David finally said. "You have your friends now. You don't need me."

"I was looking for you," I tried.

"Why?"

"It doesn't matter anymore."

And I realized, it didn't. All my worries about Charlie and the note vanished, and I crept closer. David didn't stop me this time and, finally, I stood beside him. One of the blue caps whispered to me, "Watch him, kid. We'll go for help."

"What do you care?" David demanded. "Get out!"

The blue caps slipped away, their feet slowing as they reached the stairs.

David seemed to relax. He turned back to me. His eyes were deep green, and he gazed at me until I edged to the wall's near side. Would he really jump? Or was he just screwing around? The cement burned my arm. The distance between us, only inches, could have been miles. Below, the blue caps reached ground and ran for the administration building.

"What are you doing here?" David said.

And suddenly, everything swam before me, Charlie, Meat, Amanda, the mailboxes, the ficus tree, Binky's weeping Madonna, Mrs. Blanco, so happy I'd come to visit her son, her words, *David's mentioned you.* Oh, God. He wasn't a bad guy. We might have been friends if I hadn't found Charlie. And I didn't have to ask if he'd jump. He would. This is what Gate did to people. It ate them alive. It could have eaten me.

I said, "Please, don't do this."

"Why not?" Scornful.

"Please don't," I repeated. I looked down. The sidewalk swam below, darkened by tentacly tree shadows. Then up. The tattoo on David's arm was a broken heart.

"I can't handle two more years here," he said.

"You could transfer schools."

"No, I couldn't."

"Why the hell not?"

"My parents. They have all these dreams . . ." He changed his grip on the wall. "Mom, she dishes chili mac like a grub so I can have this *exclusive* education . . . I couldn't disappoint her. Dad either."

"You think killing yourself won't disappoint them?"

"Maybe. But I won't be around to see it." He started to turn, to face outward, readying himself to jump.

"Wait!" Across campus, the two blue caps entered the administration building. They'd get someone, the police, fire rescue. There were people who talked down jumpers. I just had to stall him.

So I said, "Got the note you sent me."

"What note?"

"You know. The note about . . ." I stopped, not wanting to mention the dog. Not now.

I didn't have to. "I never sent you any note," David said.

"Sorry. Someone sent me a note. I thought it was you."

"So that's why you're here? To talk about yourself?"

"No. I heard you scream. I want to . . . help you." The sun had ducked behind a cloud, and I was cold. I said, "Why are you doing this?"

"You ever hear the story about the bat, the birds, and the beasts?"

"No."

"It's one of Aesop's fables. Mama—my mother—used to read them when I was little. Before we came here."

"Yeah, we read those too," I said. "But I don't remember that one." Was he buying time? Maybe I was wrong. Maybe he wouldn't really jump. He seemed too calm. "Tell me," I said.

David held the wall. His voice was quiet, resigned.

"Once, all the creatures lived in harmony. Then, there was

a conflict between the birds and the beasts. They formed two armies."

In the distance I heard a siren, but it passed by.

"The bat went to join with the birds. But they said, 'Sorry. You're no bird.' So, he went to join the beasts, but they said, 'You can fly. You must be a bird.'" David looked at the ground, and for a second I pictured him, soaring above it, then plummeting. "Finally, the birds and beasts made their peace. They had something in common—they all hated the bat, who was different from everyone. So the bat was forced to fly off alone before the other creatures ripped him apart."

I looked out, across campus. Principal Meeks left his office with the two blue caps. A few others followed him. David kept talking, oblivious.

"The moral is: If you aren't like anyone, you'll always be alone."

I heard Charlie's voice: *And the moral of this story, children, is: Don't get caught.*

I stared at David. "I understand."

"Do you? Well, I'm a bat," he said. Then, looking down again, "Wanna see me fly?"

I looked down too. The scene was surreal, like a childhood memory. Other people had come with Principal Meeks, come from all over—a crowd, clustering close, but not too close. All there watching and gawking. Mom was there. Her hand met her mouth when she saw me, and she stepped toward the tower door. Principal Meeks stopped her. He opened the door and started upstairs, followed by two defensive linemen in practice gear. One guy slapped the other's upraised palm. God. They hadn't called the police. They hadn't called the police. It was up to me. Suddenly, I was terrified.

Still, I kept talking. "But the bat wasn't alone."

"He was. Don't you understand? He wasn't a bird, and he wasn't a beast."

"No," I said. "He was a bat. That's not an endangered species. There are millions of bats, billions even."

David shook his head. "Not here." And suddenly, his composure crumbled. It came out a sob. "Not here."

"Yes." I gripped his shoulder. "I'm a bat, don't you see? A bat like you. I don't want to be one of them. If you jump, it will make them happy, won't it? Add some excitement to a dull Wednesday? That's why they're all here." I gestured toward the clones below. I still hated them, I realized, more than ever. I believed what I was telling David. I *was* a bat—I didn't belong with them. And if he'd just come back over that wall, I'd stick with him from now on. "If you jump, they'll cheer." Was Principal Meeks behind me yet?

"It's too late." Now, he was faltering. "They've seen me. If I don't do it now, they'll think—"

"Who cares what they think?" I heard a light step on the stair and raised my voice—difficult, because I was out of breath. "You have to stay here, breathing their air, sitting in their classrooms, crapping on their toilets, for Christ's sake. We both do, or they win."

David looked down at the crowd. Oh, it was so far down. Some jeered, others were frozen in horror. He looked scared.

"Come back over," I whispered. "They want you to jump, but I don't. Your mother doesn't. Don't do what they want."

And he began to sob in earnest. "I . . . I don't want to die." David moved closer, hugging the wall.

Then, behind me, a flurry of movement. Strong arms fumbled against my back. A hand grabbed for David's fingers. He screamed. Someone shoved me aside, and I saw David struggle, bobble on the ledge, his wrist barely in one jock's grip. His eyes sought mine.

"You bastard!" he screamed in my face.

His free hand clawed the jock's eyes. The jock lost his grip, and David hurtled toward gray and white cement. I think his scream will always be there, hanging over Gate's oak trees. The crowd raced back to give him room.

That's when they called the police. I spent the rest of the afternoon trying to answer questions with no answers. It was eight before I went home and stumbled to bed without dinner. I didn't speak to Mom, though she tried. I didn't even call Charlie.

Only later, as I struggled to find sleep, the vision of

David's broken body haunting nearly every corner of my memory, did I realize. I still didn't know who'd sent the note. It wasn't Binky or even David. Someone else.

CHAPTER TWENTY-SEVEN

"I'm getting back together with Gray."

It took me a moment to remember who Gray was. Or to care. I stared at Amanda. Around us, people were getting their books and going to class like it was a normal day, like nothing unusual had happened. Could they not know about David? Could Amanda not know? That must be it—they didn't know.

"Paul?" Amanda's voice.

"I'm sorry. What did you say?" I asked.

"I'm getting back together with Gray."

"Oh." Seconds passed before I realized. "Oh, you mean St. John."

"Right." She smiled, touched my shoulder. "I didn't want to hurt you, Paul. It's just . . . Gray and I . . . we've been together since cotillion in grade school. He gave me my first kiss behind the cabanas at the yacht club." She removed her hand from my shoulder. "We come from more similar backgrounds than you and I."

Similar backgrounds. Well, that summed it up nicely. Someone like her didn't go for someone like me. And suddenly, I knew she did know about David. She just didn't care. None of them cared.

I said, "Whatever," and walked away.

All day, I had the same sick feeling I'd had after Mom and Dad broke up. That feeling there's something wrong. You should do something. Then, you realize there's nothing to do.

I don't know how I expected Gate to deal with David's suicide. They dealt with it like they dealt with everything, by not dealing with it. I'd read about school disasters where they had grief counselors and stuff to help students. Not here. Not even a mention in the morning announcements. Was I the only one feeling grief about David? I remembered Binky's words, *David Blanco isn't one of them.* After what Amanda had said, I knew I wasn't either.

Waiting in line at Mickey D's that day, Meat tapped me on the shoulder.

"Hey, Richmond," he said. "What's red and green and definitely can't fly?"

I shrugged.

"David Blanco." He laughed.

I didn't move. Meat's laughter rang in my ears long after

he'd stopped laughing. He turned to Pierre to share the joke. I watched the hamburger helpers, sliding yellow-wrapped burgers onto trays. Fat dripped from the fries in the fryer. I couldn't eat. Meat shoved me forward.

"Look!" Pierre's voice behind me broke my daze.

I turned. We all did.

Pierre pointed toward the window. "Look, up in the sky. It's a bird!"

Another guy took it up. "It's a plane!"

Both looked up, then down, saying in unison. "Nope. It's just David Blanco."

I'm a bat. Wanna see me fly?

I was in front by then, the tall, skinny counter guy staring at me. I just stared back. I hadn't had breakfast or dinner the night before. I'd been crazy to think I could eat lunch. From his spot in the next line, Charlie nudged me. "You okay, Einstein?"

"Yeah." Though my stomach ached.

Charlie looked at the counter guy. "He'll just have a Coke, okay?" He dug into his wallet for the money to pay. I didn't protest. The guy handed Charlie the Coke. Charlie put it onto his tray and led me away, pushing my elbow with his free hand. My head was whirling. How embarrassing would it be if I fainted, and Charlie had to catch me?

He led me to a table away from the others. We sat. "Do you need to puke?" he said.

"I'm okay."

He handed me the Coke. It still fizzed. "Mary says it's good for the stomach. She used to give me Coke syrup when I was sick as a kid." He sort of smiled, remembering. "That was when she wasn't working—back when I still called her Mommy."

I nodded. My mother had done the same. Charlie tapped the cup, like the patient father, and I took a sip. It was so sweet, too sweet. The bubbles hurt my throat.

Charlie gestured toward Meat and Pierre and the others. "They're assholes, huh?" When I didn't answer, he said, "Bet it was weird, being with him when he did it."

I hadn't been sure Charlie had known I was there. But I'd forgotten—Charlie knew everything. I took another sip. The sweet hurt felt good now. "Yeah."

Charlie hadn't touched his chicken sandwich. Was he sick too? Because of David? He said, "He must have been in so much pain."

I'd been trying not to think about it. "Do you think he felt it? I mean, I figured the impact killed him."

"I don't mean when he died. I mean before. To do something like that . . . he must really have been hurting bad. And no one knew it." Charlie gestured toward our friends again. "Those guys . . . they don't understand that kind of pain, do they? They're Teflon. Nothing ever hurts them."

In my head, I heard Pierre's voice again, *It's a bird! It's a plane!* And David's, *Wanna see me fly*? I nodded, hating Pierre, hating all of them.

"But you and I know, don't we, Paul? We know what it's like to hurt. Don't we?"

"Yes." A whisper.

Charlie stood and walked to the brimming garbage pail, shoved his uneaten lunch inside, then, gesturing for me to follow, walked to the door. He stopped by Meat's table. "I'm driving Paul home. He's sick."

Once outside, Charlie called the school office on his cell phone. "No, he's okay, Mrs. Richmond . . . stomach flu, maybe . . . No, I don't think you need to leave work. I'll take him home. We're at lunch now." He looked at me, covering the mouthpiece with his hand. "Want to talk to her?" he mouthed. I shook my head. Charlie went back to the telephone. "He's lying down now . . . Yes, in the backseat. I'll have him call you later." Then, "You're welcome, Mrs. Richmond . . . Paul's a good friend to me, too."

He hung up and started driving. We were headed for his house.

"I don't want to leave you alone when you're sick," he explained. "I have to go back—got a test in religion. But Rosita will be here if you need anything. You can lie down or do your homework in my room. I'll come back after school."

I nodded. God, he was being so nice to me.

We drove in silence. I closed my eyes, feeling my head

throbbing. We were pulling into Charlie's driveway when he spoke again:

"Know what I wish sometimes?"

"What?"

"I wish something would happen to them. You know, not really hurt them, but just something to make their lives a little less . . . perfect. Maybe make them less sure of themselves for once. Does that make me a bad person?"

I shook my head. I'd been thinking the same thing all day.

"Sure it does," Charlie said. "Bet you never wish that kind of thing."

I didn't even have to think about it. I said, "Yeah, I do."

My stomach felt a little better.

CHAPTER TWENTY-EIGHT

I ended up agreeing to what Charlie wanted. He was right, of course. It wouldn't be a big deal. And even if it was, I wanted it too—now.

After Charlie left, I tried to sleep. But each time I closed my eyes, I saw David, David falling. I heard his scream. I saw his blood, his brains on the pavement. Then, I saw Pierre and the others—even Meat, whom I'd thought was nice—laughing about it.

And I heard Charlie's words: *I wish something would happen to them . . . something to make their lives a little less perfect.*

I don't know if I ever slept. But an hour after Charlie left, I logged on to his computer and opened the website with the bomb instructions. That's how Charlie found me when he got home.

"Feeling any better?" he asked.

I started, turned to look. He was smiling, not a broad grin. Just a little smile. Still concerned.

"Yeah." I gestured toward the monitor, the website. "I was thinking about it. I mean, if you're sure no one will get hurt. If it's just to scare them."

"Relax, Paul. Have I ever steered you wrong?"

I shook my head no. He never had.

We spent the rest of the afternoon planning. We'd do it Saturday night. No one would be around. Turned out, Charlie had done the groundwork, planning on setting the bomb, even without me. "But it will be more fun together," he said. He'd gathered the materials, like a two-liter soda bottle. He'd even stolen a fuse from the hardware store.

"Why steal it?" I asked when he showed it to me. "Couldn't we just buy it?" It didn't seem like stealing helped our situation any if we got caught.

Charlie stared at me over his sunglass tops. "You never watch the news, do you? Whenever there's a bomb scare or something, it always gets screwed up because some sales clerk remembers selling something to the guy. That's how they caught McVeigh."

I nodded. I didn't put us in the same category as terrorists, though. I mean, McVeigh had killed people, lots of people. Killed babies, for God's sake.

"We're not killing anyone, though," I said.

"'Course not," Charlie said. "We're just going to scare the hell out of them—like they deserve. That's what you want, right?"

I did. I wanted to terrify them. Maybe fear of their own

death would affect them as David's hadn't. Maybe it would make them less certain of their wonderful futures. I wanted *them* to justify despair. Part of me knew it was crazy, thinking that way. But, I reminded myself, no one would get hurt. Charlie had promised.

I read the instructions for about the hundredth time. They said to place the bomb in the fluorescent ceiling lights. It detonated when someone flipped the switch.

"But then, someone has to set it off. Couldn't we just—?"

"What? Light a fire and run?" Downstairs, the front door opened. Charlie heard it too and threw the fuses and stuff into the desk drawer, out of sight. "You want to be there when the fire starts?" he whispered.

I shook my head.

"Yeah, well, me neither. This way, we'll be in chapel. They'll all see it and pee their pants, but no one will get hurt. They just won't feel so safe anymore. Old Carlos comes in early and turns on the lights while everyone else is praying."

"But Old Carlos . . ." I felt sick again. Old Carlos was the last one I wanted to hurt.

"Relax." Charlie held up a hand. I heard footsteps downstairs. "There's a time-delay built in. The light has to heat up, and Old Carlos will hightail it before it burns."

That was true. I'd seen him turn on all the lights, then head back home for a smoke or something. Kids at Gate joked about how lazy he was.

I said, "I don't know. It's still a bomb." I looked at Charlie.

I knew it sounded like I didn't trust him. But I did. He was my best friend.

"Don't worry. No one's getting hurt. And if someone does . . ."

"What?"

He started toward the door, gesturing for me to follow. "No one's getting hurt." He threw the door open. "Why don't you stick around? Rosita's making paella. You could do your homework on the computer while I practice."

"Sure." Inexplicably, I felt my stomach twitch.

We went downstairs. Charlie opened the hall closet and took out his favorite racket. He had four or five, but he mostly used that one. The Hammer, he called it. "Need to call your mom?"

"Yeah." I started toward the portable phone. I turned back. "Charlie?"

He looked up.

"What you told me that time? About your dad?"

He glanced outside, checking whether his father was around. On the court, Big Chuck pointed at his watch. Charlie said, "What about it?"

"Nothing. Just, my parents are weird too."

For a second, he stood, twisting his mouth side to side, and I thought he'd say he had to go. Why was I bugging him with my problems? Then, his expression became a smile. "Yeah. I figured that out."

"You did?" I knew he'd known the obvious things—

Mom's job and the crummy place we lived. But what else?

"That stuff doesn't matter, Einstein. What matters is loyalty, having friends who'd do anything for you, no matter what."

I nodded, started toward the telephone again. I heard myself say, "Is that why you were friends with David Blanco, too?"

It was a moon ball. He'd never mentioned David. I figured he'd laugh, say what did he know about that loser. But he said, "Sort of. He turned out not to be that good a friend, though, not best friends like we are." A pained look crossed his face. "God, it's so weird that he's dead."

But I was still on *best friends*. I'd been considering Charlie my best friend for a while, but he'd never said it. I probably should have asked him about the note then. But I didn't have to. Charlie had nothing to do with it. It was so obviously Binky, screwing with me.

"Anyway." Charlie glanced outside again, bored with me, and mimed a two-handed backhand. "I have to practice."

I didn't bother calling home.

The next day, Friday, I still felt a little sick. I didn't go to school. So, I didn't see Charlie again until Saturday, hours before we planned to do it.

CHAPTER TWENTY-NINE

"You'll sleep over at my house," Charlie had said. And, of course, I'd agreed.

I didn't ask Mom's permission. I was beyond that. I just said, "I'm staying at Charlie's."

She gazed at me a second before saying, "Please don't go, Paul."

She reached to pluck a hair. Fine. Let her go bald. I met her eyes.

"He's waiting downstairs," I said.

She didn't try to stop me.

We were celebrating that night. Charlie had won his tournament that afternoon, and Mrs. Good was out of town, so Big Chuck took us to Friday's for dinner. He ordered spiked drinks, sneaking them to Charlie and me when the waitress left and taking them back when we finished. "My boys deserve a treat," he said, crunching Charlie's shoulder with one hand, mine with the other. I was flying. Music pulsated off walls, off hanging saxophones and sleds, my brain. Other people's conversations filled my head's acoustics. But I knew that tonight, all voices would go silent except Charlie's.

"How's Mandy?" Charlie asked. And, the way he said it, I knew he was roasted (one of my new words, from Meat) too.

"She doesn't like me anymore." I figured he knew she was back with St. John. I mean, Charlie knew everything.

"Maybe we'll put a little gasoline in her locker," Charlie joked. Then, he glanced at Big Chuck and mimed, *Shhhhhhh.*

We fell back into silence. Big Chuck was happy. He was drinking real drinks now, drinks without cute Friday's names or ice cream in them, and I wondered how we'd get home. I looked back at Charlie. He seemed unconcerned, so I was, too.

"You boys are quiet tonight," Big Chuck yelled over the din. "When I was younger, I used to go wild on Friday nights."

"Just reviewing the match," Charlie said. Even drunk, he knew what to say.

"That's my boy." Big Chuck chomped his steak-on-a-stick. "You're doing big things, Charlie. Big things."

"Maybe I'll do something bigger than tennis."

Mr. Good spoke through half-chewed meat. "Nothing's bigger than tennis."

Behind his glass, Charlie rolled his eyes.

Later, I lay in my sleeping bag on Charlie's floor. The air was cool, dark. Down the hall, running water, a long fart. A flush. The drone of television news turning into Letterman's Top Ten list. Then, even that ended, and there was only the stop-start of central air, Charlie's breathing above me.

Finally, a whisper. "You awake?"

"Yeah."

"Let's blaze."

I rose in the silent darkness. We'd stayed dressed, needing only shoes. These we carried over our hands, stealing downstairs, through the living room, then out the front door, not bothering to lock it. I fumbled with my sneakers, lost the tongue beneath my foot, my fingers too stiff to lace them. Charlie stood above me, frowning, his eyes empty. Finally, I got the shoes on and we walked through the soft, mulched grass that clung to our shoes and ankles.

We'd parked the bicycles on the side of the house. It was too risky to drive, Charlie had said. Instead, we pedaled through the streets. It was hot. My backpack straps strained against my shoulders. The soda bottle thumped my back. A Coke bottle, making me think about what Charlie had said about moms and Coke syrup.

We said nothing, riding miles, miles until sweat clogged my pores and ran down my back. Sometimes, there was light, streetlamps, porch lights. Usually, black branches covered the moon. We reached the school's street. My legs were pudding beneath me. I stood on the bike, willing myself to pedal. I couldn't.

"Come on." Charlie's voice in the dark. He'd ridden back around to meet me.

"I can't."

"You're wimping out?"

I said nothing. Suddenly, I was terrified.

"We're doing nothing wrong." Charlie circled behind, then ahead. "And you hate this place more than I do."

The word *hate* hung like humidity in the silent air. We'd never said anything about hating the place, about wanting to do serious damage. It was just about scaring them. And fixing Charlie's science grade. Still, I thought about the people I hung with, a lot of the same people who'd made my life miserable when I started Gate, and I knew Charlie was right. I'd do it. It would feel good to destroy at least a little part of the place—as long as no one got hurt. My legs gelled, started moving again. Then, we were there, hiding the bikes in the bushes, hoisting ourselves over the fence, the hedge, barely feeling the bougainvillea scratching our arms. Charlie joined me this time. "Wouldn't miss it," he'd said. The parking lot was just as dark, but my legs felt light. No fear. I was with Charlie now.

It was easy finding the building this time, easy to use a hairpin to jimmy the flimsy lock. I started to wipe away my fingerprints.

"Don't bother," Charlie whispered.

"Why not?"

He pushed me forward, into the room. "It's no big deal. There's a million fingerprints on that knob."

He was right, of course. And it was too late to protest anyway. We were inside. Charlie opened Zaller's file cabinet with his foot, snagged the file with his name on it.

I thought for a second about telling Charlie to just take the file. That would be enough to fix Charlie's grade.

But no. I wanted the other part, I realized. I wanted it as much as Charlie did. I wanted to be strong for once in my life. It wasn't just about Charlie's strength, but my own.

Then, Charlie was directing me to pull a desk to the room's center.

But it wasn't me who planted the bomb in the fluorescent light. Not really. It was someone else, everyone else maybe. Charlie, of course. And Mom. Binky. And David Blanco, his face smashed and bloody. And Pierre and Meat, laughing about it. And mostly Dad, because I wouldn't even have been there if he'd cared enough. They were all there with me. Maybe Pierre held the flashlight while the others clambered onto one another's backs to the ceiling. Binky was the lookout. Mom drew the panel away from the light. David held the gas-filled bottle because he had nothing to lose. Dad rigged the fuse. It couldn't have been just me. And Charlie, holding the flashlight while I stood in the light column, then climbed atop the desk I'd pulled out. "You have to do it," Charlie said. "You're taller." And I was. And I did it. But not just me.

"Watch out," Charlie said.

A glance down. Odor met my nostrils. Gas. Charlie shone his light on the black pool. "Should we clean it?" I asked.

"No, it will evaporate. Just finish."

I looked up again, and Dad's hand slid the panel back in place. He didn't look at me. Dad never looked at me.

"No one's getting hurt," a voice—Charlie's—intoned.

I climbed down.

"And if they do," the voice continued, "who cares?"

"Who cares?" I repeated.

Then, I was back in my sleeping bag in Charlie's room. The tile felt hard, bumpy beneath me. And cold. Across the room, the wood-slatted blinds let in the seeping starlight. I watched it grow lighter, brighter, invading my pupils so I had to close my eyes. I didn't sleep. Above me, in the comfort of his bed, Charlie breathed evenly, childlike, sleeping the sleep of the righteous.

CHAPTER THIRTY

Monday, 8:05. I sat on my hands in chapel. I sat alone, too, watching Charlie and Meat arrive after me and take seats in the opposite pew. I couldn't catch Charlie's eye. Was he ignoring me? Reverend Phelps called us to worship. The choir started its first deafening hymn. I waited, listening through their singing for the sound. Any second. Class started at eight twenty-five. By then, it would all be over.

8:10. Amanda came in late. Just about everyone turned to watch her walk down the aisle, hair flaming. The color of temptation. The choir was singing:

Heavy is my tribulation,
Sore my punishment has been,
Broken by thine indignation,
I am troubled by my sin.

She sat across the aisle. St. John scooted close to her.

8:11. A senior I didn't know was doing the reading. It was "If Thy Arm Offend Thee, Cut It Off." I barely heard it. Was that a siren screaming? Stupid. Just a sour note on the organ.

Why hadn't it gone off?

Mom sat with the office staff. After chapel, she'd go back to the classroom building. I remembered her, Saturday, saying, *Please don't go, Paul.*

The bomb still hadn't gone off. The bomb still hadn't gone off!

It was a dud, I told myself. It just didn't work. But I knew. No one had turned on the lights yet. It would go off when everyone got to class.

8:14. Reverend Phelps was praying.

Forgive us our trespasses as we forgive those . . .

Oh, God.

And lead us not into temptation, but deliver us from evil.

I twisted to look at Charlie. He sat, hands in lap, neat. Innocent. When I turned back, Reverend Phelps was glaring at me. But still, he was praying. He'd finished the Lord's Prayer and prayed for a litany of other things, the academic success of Gate's students, the victories of our sports teams, the warmth of our school lunches.

"And Lord, help us find another family to assist in the caretaking duties of the school." A chance line, thrown in. Reverend Phelps continued, praying for the grass to grow, the weeds to die.

I nudged the kid beside me. "What did he say?"

The kid shook his head. "He said a lot—too much."

"About caretaking duties?"

He didn't answer. I knew the reverend was looking at me, but I had to know. I had to know. I didn't look up. I nudged the kid again.

The kid said, "Guess they're still looking for someone to replace Old Carlos."

"Replace?" A hiss. *Still?*

The kid didn't answer. I nudged him harder. Finally, he whispered. "He left Friday—okay? He and his wife. They just took their stuff and cleared out."

Cleared out. Because of David, of course. Of course. I'd missed Friday. But Charlie had been there, and Charlie knew everything. Charlie knew Old Carlos was gone, knew there was no janitor to turn on the lights. He'd lied to me! He'd lied to me! I rose without realizing it and threw my hymnal to the pew. I had to go. If Old Carlos wasn't there, Zaller would be the one to open the door. Zaller, and everyone in her class. I couldn't let that happen. I'd only wanted to scare people, not hurt them. Not kill them. I could hear it already, above the choir. Screaming. I shoved the kid back and ran up the aisle, past the startled seventh graders and out the heavy wood-and-glass door.

A rush of cool air hit my face. The hissing sound of trees. Then, silence. And my own breath. I stopped a second, couldn't move. I checked my watch—8:16.

"Where are you going?"

It was Charlie. Charlie behind me. I didn't hesitate. "To Zaller's room. To stop her." I started forward again.

Charlie's voice stopped me. "Why would you do that?"

"I don't want anyone hurt." I knew that was right. I started walking again. Charlie followed me closer to the main building.

"No one's getting hurt, Paul. We were just screwing around. It'll set off the sprinkler system."

I wanted to say something about him knowing Old Carlos wasn't there, but I didn't. I didn't have time to fight with him.

So, I said, "Look, it was a stupid idea, Charlie." I thought I knew what his problem was, so I said, "I won't get you in trouble. They won't notice the missing file right away. We could do something about it, but—"

His tennis-enhanced arm grabbed mine. "This isn't about the file anymore."

Still, I tried to walk away.

"I thought you knew that, but apparently, you're really that stupid." Charlie's voice was flat. Behind me, I could still hear the outline of Reverend Phelps's shouting. "This is much bigger than the file. We're in deep shit if you tell." For a second, his face wasn't Charlie's face at all. It was scary.

"It *is* a big deal, Charlie. Really big. People could get hurt." He didn't understand, and I couldn't make him, so I walked, pulling him with me. He was strong, but I was bigger, and finally, I pulled away. "I can't do this." I was yelling, not caring who heard now. "People could get hurt."

Then, I turned my back on him. I'd never done that before. I walked down the gravel path toward the oaks that divided the chapel from the main building. 8:17. The sun blazed through the cool air like fire, fire in my mind, fire maybe everywhere if I didn't stop it from happening. I had to go. Had to get away from Charlie. Had to stop it. But again, Charlie's voice stopped me.

"Think you'll be a hero?"

I didn't, couldn't speak. His voice joined me again, there like the air.

"Think they'll pin some medal on you when you tell? Good old Paul, plants a bomb, then saves us from it. Think they'll be grateful? No way. You'll be expelled. We'll both be expelled. And your mother will be fired from her pathetic job."

"I didn't want to be a hero. I never wanted to be a hero." *I just wanted to be your friend.*

He laughed. "Well, good, because you won't be. Think anyone will believe you didn't know that bomb could hurt people? Do you even really believe that?"

His voice was barely audible through the tree-winds. His face was dead calm.

I stared at him. Close as he was, I had to look down to do

it. Except you never looked down at Charlie, not really.

"Did you really think you could plant a bomb full of gasoline in a school full of people and no one would get hurt?"

I couldn't respond.

"Well?"

"I thought . . ."

I started to repeat that I'd thought it would go off with no one there. But I wondered. Had I? Had I really? And the horror of what could happen, would happen, unfolded before my eyes. Why *had* I done it?

"I don't know," I said, answering Charlie's question and my own.

Charlie smiled then. "It doesn't matter whether you do or not, Paul. You won't do anything about it, won't screw up your life worse than it already is. Will you?"

I shook my head. Behind me, the choir started "Onward Christian Soldiers," which always ended chapel. I glanced at my watch. Nineteen after. The numbers switched. 8:20. "You're wrong, Charlie."

But his eyes held me there. "Do yourself a favor," he said. "Skip class. Go to the beach, or go home, but this is real. It's happening because we made it happen. You wanted it as much as I did."

I heard the organ thumping the final beats. Then, just the wind in the oaks. It was too late to do anything now.

Finally, I said, "All right, Charlie. Okay."

"Good man."

I turned for the last time and started back toward chapel. But the doors were open, and a plaid ocean rolled forward, swarming toward fate. Behind me, Charlie yelled, "Go the other way, Einstein!" He was headed for his first class, in a portable on the other side of campus. I turned to do his bidding once again. I knew, as Charlie had said, something would happen. Something big. And, like Charlie, I wanted to be somewhere else when it did.

I cut across the grass toward the athletic field. I saw Binky and stopped.

I couldn't say why I stopped. We hadn't spoken in weeks. She hated me. But somehow, Binky was the only one I cared about. Binky had Zaller first period. I'd sort of put that out of my mind before. But now, she would be there when it happened. The explosion could kill someone. I ran back, the grass chafing against my shoes. "I'm skipping," I said. "Come with me." I checked my watch. Twenty-two after. Chapel had ended late.

She looked at me like I'd peed my pants or something. "Not likely." She kept walking.

I grabbed her wrist. "I'm serious. Come with me."

"Go away!"

She was strong for a girl, but still, I struggled against her. "Please. Just this once, trust me." We'd entered the main building, the opposite of where I wanted to go. I gripped her arm harder. "Please. Just—"

"Mr. Richmond!"

We turned. Principal Meeks stood before us. He didn't smile. "No time for love scenes, children. Reverend Phelps was a bit long-winded today." He nodded at Binky. "Where are you supposed to be, Miss . . ."

"Zaller. I was just going." Binky pulled away from me and took off down the breezeway before I could speak again.

"And you, Mr. Richmond? I believe you have Mrs. Sheridan this hour?"

I nodded.

"Splendid. I'm passing her room on my way to the office. I'll escort you."

I nodded again and twisted my head to watch Binky's plaid back fade, probably forever, from sight. I couldn't believe I was going to hurt her. Maybe kill her because I was too weak, too tired to do anything else. And she'd been my only friend. Not Charlie. Not Charlie at all.

"I'm waiting, Mr. Richmond."

I followed Meeks. It didn't matter. My life was over, too.

8:24. I reached Sheridan's class. Zaller's room was at the far end of the building, near the parking lot. But someone would be there soon. Someone would open the door. I sat. And I waited, thinking about what Charlie had said Saturday night, *Something big.* So, I waited to die. Waited for an explosion. Or maybe nothing at all, something too fast to hear or notice or feel. Would the end come instantly, in a cloud of smoke, a hail of flying bodies? Or slowly, in a fire that rolled across the buildings, taking lives as it went, taking my own life while, safely across campus, Charlie Good diagrammed sentences in a portable classroom?

8:25. Nothing. 8:26. Nothing. Sheridan started class. I relaxed. Maybe I'd been wrong. Maybe it was just a small fire.

Then, sirens in the distance.

Lots of sirens.

And the fire alarm, clanging, loud and rough through the whispering trees.

And Principal Meeks over the intercom.

"Students! Please evacuate the building! This is not a drill! Leave your books on your desks and exit in an orderly fashion. I repeat: This is not a drill!"

Then, silence. And the screaming faces around me.

CHAPTER THIRTY-ONE

They evacuated us to the athletic field. It was drizzling. The neat lines we'd practiced in monthly fire drills fell apart in actual use, fanning across campus like ants on acid. The mood ranged from impatience to exuberance to near hysteria.

I was numb.

Our class was one of the first out, so I watched the others. A seventh grader screamed in the bleacher shadows. Mrs. Nordstrom, the school nurse, led her away from the group. *Mustn't upset anyone.* Another kid was yelling at my mother. He wanted to go back to his locker to get his catcher's mitt. "It was two hundred dollars, and it's coming out of your salary." Maybe blowing this place up hadn't been such a bad idea.

Charlie stood across the field, staring over the ficus hedge. Down the street, sirens screamed, closer, closer, drowning out words, thoughts. Closer. Then, they stopped. Three fire engines, one red, two vivid lime, screamed into sight. Firefighters swarmed like maggots on day-old kill, finally heading toward the classroom building. Charlie didn't move. A frown stretched across his mouth. Someone who didn't know him might have missed it. I knew him—at least, I did now.

Binky sat Indian-style, halfway between Charlie and me. She hadn't followed instructions about leaving her books on her desk. Most people hadn't.

As if on cue, she looked up, responding to my gaze. She knew. Knew I was involved in it and knew why. I shouldn't have warned her. Now, I needed to act like it was all coincidence. Still, I couldn't look away, like we were having a staring contest, seeing who'd blink first.

Binky did. Her eyes wandered to Charlie, across the field, then back to me. She shrugged and returned to the book she was reading.

By then, the teachers had given up on keeping order, given up pretending even. Girls got on guys' shoulders to see over the hedge, and people wondered aloud if we'd get to leave. A group to one side took advantage of the break to cram for a test with homemade flash cards.

Amanda was part of that group. But when she saw me, she came over.

"You hear what happened?" When I shook my head, she said, "This place could blow sky-high, and it started in our room. Zaller's room, I mean." People had started to group around, and Amanda pulled back, making the most of her story. "We got there, and the door was locked. So, we're standing there, and Old Lady Z's fumbling with her keys." She imitated Zaller's trembling hands. "Finally, she gets us in. Then, she turns around and starts yelling to get out. She turned off the lights. That's when we noticed . . ." Amanda flipped her hair, enjoying her audience. "The place reeked of gasoline."

The gas I'd spilled. That had saved them. Saved us.

Amanda was still going. "So, she's running as much as she can, screaming at us. And Pierre Loisel's screwing around, dragging his feet until finally, Zaller just shoves him outside. Turns out . . . she thought there was a bomb in the ceiling."

She finished and stared over the hedges at the fire trucks. That was when the bomb-squad arrived.

Amanda turned back, realizing. "Oh my God. It was real, wasn't it?" She looked back at the bomb-squad guys, watching until they were sucked into the building.

Coach Kjelson and Principal Meeks were patrolling with whistles, trying to chase everyone from the bushes. People ignored them. Amanda looked at the fire trucks and obeyed their orders. I did too.

When I'd moved halfway across the field, I saw Binky again. How long had she been watching? She approached me.

"Tell me you had nothing to do with this."

"What?" I stared. "Of course not. To do with what?"

"I think you know," she said. "You warned me not to go to Zaller."

And for some reason, I relaxed. I looked her straight in the eye, hearing Charlie's voice coming from me. "I didn't know, Binky," the voice said reasonably. "I was screwing around."

Across the field, Charlie still frowned.

By noon, the rain had burned off, and Charlie had stopped ignoring me. They brought us lunch, so Charlie, Meat, and I crouched on the ground, slurping pizza. We didn't talk. The lunch ladies—all except Mrs. Blanco—were circulating, threatening to write people up if they got near the school. But it was pretty clear it wasn't blowing up, so people were bored. Someone had brought out a portable stereo, and music—I think it was Furious George—filled the air. Kids with cell phones called home. They reported back that we were on the news—only channel 7 because the networks were running soaps.

Charlie was silent. Except one time, when Meeks passed, Charlie stood. "Uh, sir?"

Meeks squared his shoulders. Then, seeing it was Charlie, his face relaxed halfway. "Yes, Charlie."

"Thank you for the pizza, sir." Charlie made eye contact. "We were all very hungry."

Meeks smiled for the first time all day. "You're welcome, Charlie." He reached to squeeze Charlie's shoulder. "Never let it be said that I'd neglect my students' needs—even in the face of this sort of conduct."

"I appreciate that, sir. We all appreciate it."

When Charlie sat again, it was closer to Meat, away from me.

Finally, they let us go. Mom was nuts all the way home, driving seventy down side streets, then slowing to a crawl for miles. She was repeating, "How could they do this?"

The old instincts kept coming back. I wanted to hug her, make it better. I couldn't. The lies I'd told fought battles with her lies. Neither won. I stayed put.

Later, I heard her in the living room making calls. Meeks had her organize a phone chain, calling parents to discuss today's "incident," reassuring them that Gate was still safe.

"They're doing everything possible to find the person responsible," I heard her say. Then, "No, it couldn't have been one of our students."

CHAPTER THIRTY-TWO

I lay awake a long time that night, waiting. Finally, I heard the knock on the window. I opened the blinds. It was Charlie.

Come down, he mouthed. I wanted to say no, but I went.

I scanned two rows of econo-boxes, identically gray in the dimness, before I found Rosita's car. Good old Charlie, blending with the locals. His windows were black in the night. Air bubbles, where the after-market tint had come up, blocked my view. Charlie rolled down the window. He didn't open the door.

"Way to ignore me today," I said.

"It was necessary," Charlie's voice replied.

"I don't get that."

"You don't get it period, Paul." Charlie's voice was sharp as the night air. "I pity you that."

I strained to see him, but only made out blond hair, bits of face. The rest was shadow. "What don't I get, Charlie?"

He ignored the question. "Mary flew home when she heard. She spoke with Meeks. As a concerned parent, not to mention a United States prosecutor, she felt entitled to information. She got it."

"What information?"

"Apparently, someone planted a bomb at Gate," Charlie said, like it was the first he'd heard about it. "A bomb with enough firepower to take out the whole wing, maybe the whole school if the wind was right. Needless to say, my parents were shocked."

I tried to nod, unable to speak. My stomach tightened, clear up to my face. The whole school. I hadn't thought it was *that* powerful. Had Charlie known? He'd done all the prep work, after all. A dark van pulled into the lot, and Charlie hissed something. I ducked, listened to it roar past. I stood. Charlie rolled his window back down.

"Normally, police won't discuss a case in progress. But Mary has connections there as well."

Okay, so you're important. Cut to the chase, Charlie. Then, I felt guilty. Maybe Charlie hadn't known about Old Carlos. Maybe he was as freaked out as I was. In any case, I had to talk to Charlie. It was good he was finding this stuff out. So, I said, "What did they tell her?" I couldn't believe the police were involved. It was supposed to be a prank.

"No leads yet." Charlie's voice from the black-hole window. "Fingerprints are worthless—whole student body's had their hand on that knob. No one saw anything, so they figure the culprit arrived on foot."

Culprit. I wiped a sweat bead from my eyelid.

"All they have is a profile."

"What's that?"

"Something police do." Charlie's voice was louder now, confident. "Try to figure out what kind of person would do this kind of thing."

"What type would?" Trying to match Charlie's bravado, like it was so cool the police were looking for us, like they'd never find out.

Charlie laughed. "He'd be a loner, they say. Type who doesn't interact well with others, hangs in the science wing or the computer lab." He turned, and for the first time, I saw his face well. "Sound like anyone you know, Paul?"

That's when I got it. Charlie had always known. He'd meant to take out half the school while he sat safely in a portable. Failing that, he'd convince them it was my idea. I was the computer whiz who knew how to use everything. Charlie didn't even have a password for the school's computer. We'd always used mine. But this hadn't been my idea. I'd only been involved at the end.

"You're trying to pin this on me?" I said.

"'Course not." His voice was calm. Good Old Charlie again.

"Sounds like it. Sounds like you're abandoning me."

"Listen!" The word was a hiss. "I'm not abandoning anyone, but this is serious." Serious, another hiss. "You can't go running out of chapel or talking to your friend, Pinky, like it's a miracle she's alive. You can't act guilty. I stand by my friends, but you can't be my friend and act stupid."

The word stung. After all we'd been through, all we'd done, I still wanted Charlie's approval. I'd never get it, I realized, any more than I'd get Dad's. I looked up at Mom's blank bedroom window, and suddenly, I was tired, so tired I could cuddle beside her and sleep through the next week of school. I stepped away from the car, ready to leave. Then, I turned back.

"*Are* we friends, Charlie?"

"Of course we are." Charlie's voice was gentle again, almost loving in the darkness. "You're the best friend I ever had, Einstein. Otherwise, I'd throw you to the wolves and move on."

And he would. I'd always known it.

I nodded, and he drove away, lights off, like a shark gliding silently through the night ocean.

CHAPTER THIRTY-THREE

Everything seemed almost normal the next morning. Almost. In religion class, it was more like a Monday, because across the aisle, Kirby was enlightening everyone about the frat boy who'd tried to feel her up at a Sigma Chi party over the weekend ("Puh-leeze! Like, he was cool, but not that cool.") and Tyler James flexed in his too-small polo. Ryan Moorman, who was marginally in our lunch group, leaned over to borrow a pen, but I didn't have an extra one. I wasn't sure I'd brought *one.* Maybe they'd ignore the bomb like they'd ignored David's suicide. Maybe everything was okay.

But David's death hadn't affected them. This did.

Mrs. Sheridan looked like someone had to push her through the door. No one else noticed. They all kept flexing and talking, doing next period's homework or reading *Car and Driver.* Sheridan stood there. At five after, Meeks's voice blared over the intercom.

All teachers, please bring your classes to the gymnasium.
For the first time ever, he hadn't cleared his throat.

Meeks stood at the intersection of two green lines on the floor. It was near the spot where I'd stood the day of registration, when I'd first seen Charlie. Meeks's tie was undone. He watched us enter. Some people were talking, laughing, glad to miss class a second day. But most were quiet. And even though I hadn't wanted the bomb to go off, I was glad. Something had finally moved them when nothing else could. Meeks watched us. We filled the bleachers, some orderly, others stumbling with backpacks, running to sit with friends. Meeks's gaze saw us all. Most quieted down. Some talked on, oblivious. Meeks didn't yell for quiet or try to get anyone's attention. Just waited until we were all seated. Two police officers stood by the basketball hoop, watching, too. A few people looked at them. Most tried not to, the way you don't look at cops. Finally, Meeks's silence overtook the room. We all stared.

Meeks stared back. Did he meet my eyes? Impossible. When he started to speak, again, he didn't clear his throat.

"Something terrible has happened." He paused for us to hear it. "As you may now know, an explosive device was found in a classroom yesterday. Difficult as it is for me to believe, the police hypothesize that it was set by one of our students."

Around me, a buzz, people talking. A too-loud voice said,

"Bet it was Emily!" and people turned to look. Someone laughed.

"This is a serious matter," Meeks said, and everyone quieted down. "Mrs. Zaller entered that room with several students. But for her quick thinking, they might have been killed. Everyone in the wing might have been killed."

I looked around. Stunned faces met my gaze. And there was Charlie, atop the side bleacher, shocked as anyone. Blending in. Meeks was still speaking. He had everyone's attention now.

"Shocked and saddened as I am by this incident, I know you must be also. We need your assistance in finding this troubled, troubled student. I urge you to search your excellent memories for any clue. The police inform me that there are usually warning signs of these tendencies. Ask yourself: Have any of my classmates behaved suspiciously? Or said anything to indicate a grudge against the school or Mrs. Zaller?"

I fidgeted, thinking of Charlie's profile, then stopped myself.

"I have asked the faculty to report the name of any student absent from morning chapel yesterday. I do not wish to alarm you. Still, I will not rest until I have ferreted out this evil in our midst."

Evil. I turned the word over in my mind. But what did it mean?

Meeks turned toward an upraised hand. "Yes?"

Everyone looked to see who it was. I did too.

It was Binky. Binky, who never spoke in class, much less in front of the whole school. She glanced around. Finally, she said, "What would happen, I mean, to the person who did this?"

"An excellent question, Miss . . . yes, uh, Miss . . ." Binky didn't help him. She was ranked first in our class, yet Meeks didn't know her name. Unbelievable. Finally, he said, "Unfortunately, it's a question I'm not qualified to answer. However, I assure you that any person who would do such a thing is deeply troubled and in need of help." Meeks nodded for emphasis. "Your reporting their tendencies would only be to their benefit."

Binky didn't respond, and Meeks dismissed us. We walked in silence. Somehow, I was in front, and I pushed through the yellow-painted metal door, its cold hardness resisting my shoulder. Everyone followed, fanning out to the classrooms, taking their seats in silence. I didn't open my religion book, just sat while, around me, everyone else fumbled with their backpacks.

Then, Tyler's voice boomed from the back. "All right, who's the psycho?"

A few people laughed. But it was a nervous laugh.

Somehow, I got through the morning. I talked to the usual people—Charlie's friends. It was pretty much like other days. But I felt like something was waiting behind me. Or above my head, like the raven in the Edgar Allan Poe poem, quothing *Nevermore*, whatever that meant, and ready to swoop. And maybe it was better that Meeks called me in at the end of fourth period, before lunch. Because I wouldn't have gotten through lunch anyway, not knowing. Not knowing was worse than anything. And when the office volunteer came to get me from history, his feet tyrannosauruslike on the hollow-floored portable classrooms, I knew why he was there. And I was relieved.

But I was freaking by the time I got to Meeks's office. Would I be expelled? Go to jail? Could you go to jail at fifteen? I didn't think so. But Mom would definitely lose her job if I was expelled. Sure, I'd been mad at Mom, but her job was our only money. She couldn't lose it. She didn't deserve this. What had I done to her?

Calm down.

Charlie was leaving when I got to Meeks's office. Leaving—good sign. Big Chuck was with him. Bad sign. I could tell from Charlie's face he wanted to talk. Probably a good sign. Except he couldn't. Big Chuck didn't acknowledge me. He gripped Charlie's arm, supporting his son. And beyond them, Meeks sat, the American flag drooping behind him, like the president giving the State of the Union. He watched us, Charlie and me. So Charlie couldn't talk.

I thought maybe the police would be there, like they'd been at assembly. It was good they weren't, wasn't it?

"Close the door, Paul."

Meeks's voice grabbed me. I moved toward it, then back to shut the door. I'd never seen his office before. I stopped a second, entranced by the doorknob, shiny yellow brass, not like the cheap brushed chrome knobs on the other doors. My mind was doing ninety. What had Charlie said? What had Meeks asked? My story had to match Charlie's, but what had he said?

Chill. Meat's word. Charlie had said nothing.

"Have a seat, Paul."

Even my name sounded wrong. Meeks usually called everyone Mr. or Miss. Still, I decided Charlie had denied it. He was walking away, wasn't he? I'd deny it too. They knew nothing, or the police would be here. The lighting made me squint. I looked down.

"I've meant to call you in for a while, Paul."

Hope tickled my heart. Maybe this wasn't about the bomb at all then. Please, let it not be about the bomb. If I could get away with this one thing, I'd never do anything wrong again. I said, "You have?"

"Yes. Since the Blanco boy's death. Unfortunate business. You had a part in that, I know."

Relief flooded me like sunlight. I tried not to grin. This wasn't about the bomb. It wasn't about the bomb. I didn't think to wonder why he wanted to see me about

David's suicide. I'd had nothing to do with that. I'd been an innocent bystander.

"Paul?"

"Well, I was there, sir."

"Yes." Meeks's fingers played here-is-the-steeple. "We were deeply saddened by the incident, deeply saddened. Still, your mother is an excellent employee, and we'd had no other problems with you."

Open the doors. Here are the people.

"Paul?"

Problems with me? Was he blaming me for David's suicide? Impossible.

"We saw your friendship with Charlie Good as an excellent sign," Meeks said.

The steepled fingers went flat. He *was* blaming me.

"I barely knew David Blanco, sir."

"No?" His eyes didn't believe me. "And yet, you were with him when he took his life. And now, another incident where it seems you were involved." Meeks's eyes wandered to the window. Mine did, too, saw what his saw, Charlie and his father leaving out the downstairs exit.

"Incident?" Downstairs, classes were changing. It should have been too far to hear, but I did, every conversation and laugh, all those feet walking, running, swarming like flies on a dead man's eyes.

"I think you know, Paul." The noise stopped, and I heard Meeks's voice. "The bomb in Mrs. Zaller's room. His eyes

223

returned to me. "We wanted to give you the benefit of the doubt. That's why we spoke with Charlie first."

"Charlie told you I was involved?"

"Were you involved, Paul?"

"What did Charlie say?"

Meeks's fingers rose again. "Charlie told us all we needed to know."

I stared at him, realizing. Charlie had ratted me out. Gave me up to keep himself out of trouble. I felt something in my throat, bile, and clapped a hand to my mouth. My head was pounding, pounding. Meeks yelled, "Come in!" and I realized it was the door. But it kept on.

Rhonda, Meeks's secretary, stuck her head in. "Mrs. Richmond is here."

Mom rushed in. Could she stop me from puking, screaming? But she was pulling hairs, saying, "Oh, Paul," over and over, pulling, pulling her hair. And I felt sicker at how much I'd hurt her. She was my mother, after all. I began to cough, cry before I could stop myself, and before I could stop myself, my words came like puke. "It wasn't just me. Shit. It was Charlie's idea, Charlie and I. But I didn't want to hurt anyone. I mean, it wasn't just me. I didn't want to hurt anyone."

And Meeks stared at me. Mom stopped talking, stopped pulling, and they both stared. And finally, Meeks said, "Charlie said neither of you had anything to do with it. He knew nothing about it."

But I couldn't stop crying.

CHAPTER THIRTY-FOUR

It was like I'd broken a gasket and I couldn't stop crying or talking or get fixed. I cried all afternoon and on and off the next week. And somewhere in the middle, I told the whole story. About Charlie and changing the grade in the computer, the Mailbox Club, the bagels. And the bomb. Meanwhile, the police were working.

First thing, they got a search warrant and took Charlie's computer. That was my fault. I'd told them we'd gotten the bomb instructions off the Internet.

The day they took it, Charlie came over our apartment. He must have taken a bus. At least, I didn't see his car in the parking lot or even Rosita's. But when I heard the knock on the door, I knew. Who else would be coming to see me?

Our apartment was empty. Mom was still working at Gate. She said it's hard to replace someone midterm, though she guessed they'd probably can her over Christmas. Of course, Meeks had asked that I not return. So I was home alone when Charlie stepped into our narrow front hall. I didn't worry about our door, white paint flaking to reveal beige underneath, the pitted cement in the breezeway or our molting doormat. I was through worrying about what people—Charlie, especially—thought.

Charlie stepped inside. Mom had bought our Christmas tree the morning Charlie and I planted the bomb. I'd refused to go with her. She'd brought it back by herself. It was $19.95 at Target, and she'd said it would look big in our tiny place. It didn't. The tree was dotted with tinsel and a few lights and awful things we'd made over the years from clothespins and balsa wood. I hadn't helped put it up. I was sorry about that now. Still, the pine scent decorated the room. Charlie sat, looking like he belonged there, blending in.

"They took my computer," he said.

"Yeah, I know."

"Maybe they won't find anything," he said. "I mean, you cleaned it out, right—the temporary Internet files, the cookies?" He could have looked up, then, for reassurance. He didn't. He didn't need *my* reassurance.

And I didn't give it to him. "They'll find something," I said. "You can't completely delete stuff. It's there if they look hard enough."

He leaned back, putting his tennis shoes—always his tennis shoes—onto the stack of *Ladies' Home Journal*s on our coffee table. *Couldn't you just look scared, Charlie? Be human for once?*

He still didn't look at me. "Why'd you do it, Paul?"

"Do what, Charlie? Listen to you?"

"Come off it." He stared at the horrible Christmas tree. "Why'd you tell? We were riding this out."

I panicked, I wanted to say. But I didn't. Even now, I couldn't admit that to him. "They'd have found out anyway," I said instead.

"Glad you're so sure." Still gazing at the tree.

Look at me, you bastard. I wanted to grab his face, make him look. He'd used me and now, I knew it. "You're blaming me for this?"

He met my eyes finally. "See anyone else around?"

"Yeah, Charlie. I see you. I'd never have done this without you."

I heard something then, a low chuckle from the back of his throat. "Without me," he said. "Is that what you'll tell them, Paul? Is that what you tell yourself—I made you? Charlie Good took your innocent baby hands and made them plant the bomb?"

"You got me to do stuff I'd never have considered." I stared at him, silhouetted in the sun filtered through the Gumbo Limbo trees and our blinds. He said nothing, so I added, "It's true."

"You could have said no."

I started at his words. The pine was stronger, choking me. And something else. The realization that he was right. I could have said no. I could have said no, but I hadn't. No matter what Charlie had done, I could always have said no.

Why hadn't I? Because I'd wanted to be cool for Charlie? No, not just that. Because I'd *wanted* to do it. In that way, I was no different than Charlie. The realization terrified me.

"David Blanco said no," Charlie said. Then, he laughed at the incredulous look on my face. "Pretty sad, when the kid who offs himself has more inner strength than you. But then, you wanted to go along with me. You wanted so badly to be part of the cool group."

"You asked David to do this?"

Charlie shrugged. "Needed someone with access to the building keys."

"And that's why we were friends? Were we ever really friends?"

"Don't get self-righteous, Paul. Like I said, we all use one another. You used me, maybe more than I used you." Then, his face softened. Good old Charlie. "No, it's not why. You know that. You were my best friend, Einstein. You were the best friend I ever had. The only person I'm closer to is my dad."

I started at the word. "Your dad? You mean, Big Chuck?"

"The great man himself."

"But I thought . . ." Suddenly, my whole stomach felt weak. "You said you were scared of him. That he wasn't really your dad, and you had to kill yourself to please him."

"You believed that?" Charlie laughed. "I was screwing

with you, Einstein. Maybe I should stop calling you that, because you aren't very smart, really. Of course Big Chuck's my real father."

I stared at him, unable to respond. Then, I realized I didn't need to. He wouldn't have listened anyway. I stood, walked to the door, opened it, and waited for him to leave. He didn't argue, just slipped past me and pressed the button for the elevator.

But there was one thing more I needed to know before he left forever.

"Who killed the dog, Charlie?"

"St. John did." Without blinking.

I stared. St. John. I guess I'd never know for sure who sent the note. Maybe even St. John himself.

"Did you . . . make him?"

"I just told you, Paul. I can't *make* anyone do anything."

I nodded, and the elevator door shut.

I sank to the floor and sat there a long time just staring at the door where Charlie had gone. I wondered who I was. And who I'd become.

CHAPTER THIRTY-FIVE

I'd been in juvenile detention a week. It felt like longer, though, because I was awake all the time. The nights were loud. The days were louder, banging, screaming, people shouting stuff at you. And sometimes, noises I didn't recognize. Those were the worst. The first night, the guy in the next bunk, a skinny kid called Hemp, told me he'd been raped when he first got there. "They look for a new piece of ass," he said. I hoped he was messing with me, but I wasn't taking any chances. So, after that, I didn't sleep, ever. I watched my back. Finally, I was glad to be big.

They'd picked me up after searching Charlie's computer. They'd found the Internet files encrypted in the hard drive. The next day, an officer was at my door, reading me my rights. Then, I was in detention. When Mom visited, she told me they'd picked Charlie up too, but I hadn't seen him. I didn't want to see him.

"Richmond!" A guard yelled my name when I was on line for breakfast.

He was short, so I looked down. It was a thin line with guards. Act too respectful, people bust your ass. I'd learned that from experience. But you didn't want them on your bad side, either. "Yeah?" I strived for the right tone.

He scowled. "Your lawyer's here."

"I don't have a lawyer, sir."

"You saying I'm seeing things?" he demanded, while, around me, guys imitated my *sir*.

"No, sir." I followed him out.

He took me to a lounge. Orange plastic furniture with stained foam rubber sticking out everywhere. Mom was there with a man I didn't recognize. She embraced me. It was a gesture I'd have refused a week before. But now, I held my face stiff to keep from bawling, *I'm sorry. I'm so sorry.* She smelled clean, like the soap from our bathroom.

"Paul, this is Mr. Rossi," Mom said. "He'll be representing you."

"How can we afford this?"

"Your father paid," Mom said. "He's quite upset about the scandal. It's in all the papers. But I hired the lawyer. I did everything myself." She nodded, proud of herself. I gaped. How had she gotten it together enough to do this for me? The answer hit me hard: She loved me.

Mom had called Dad after my confession. He hadn't

spoken to me, but I'd heard him yelling through the phone. Now, I pictured the headline: LIEUTENANT COLONEL'S SON PLANTS BOMB or whatever. I almost smiled. But I didn't. Mr. Rossi stared at me. I shuffled my feet, sticking my hand out as an afterthought.

"We'll need to work on your eye contact," he said. And I heard the echo, Big Chuck, yelling at Charlie, *Eye contact!* "You don't look at people, they think you're guilty."

"I am guilty," I said.

"Want to stay here, then?" he asked.

Down the hall, someone was getting beat up. I smelled Mom's Camay soap again and swallowed. "No."

"Then, I don't need to hear that." He didn't sit on the plastic sofa, just perched on the arm. Didn't want to dirty his pants. I sat. The orange medical-scrub-type outfit I wore was nothing I planned to keep.

"But I confessed," I said.

"We'll talk about that confession."

I looked at Mom. To my surprise, she sat calm, not pulling her hairs at all. My stomach felt empty from the breakfast I'd missed. I couldn't have eaten. My throat was too full. I looked at Mom again. I managed, "Am I getting out of here? Can I go home?"

Mr. Rossi nodded. "For now, I think so. Later . . ." He shook his head. "I don't know. Like I said, we'll discuss your confession."

"Tell him what happened." Mom said.

"Your friend's story doesn't agree with yours," Rossi said. I think he snorted when he said *friend*. "Says he first heard of the bomb the day it was found."

"What would you expect him to say?" Mom asked. And I was glad she was talking, because I couldn't.

Rossi nodded. "Problem is, the police are believing him."

I remembered what Charlie had said about the criminal profile. I fit it. Charlie didn't. Why would the golden child build a bomb? Yet he had. I'd just followed, stupidly followed.

I found my voice. "But his computer? The stuff was on his computer."

"Your friend claims you used his computer while he practiced tennis with his father. He says you were at his house alone a whole afternoon that week."

The bastard. He really had thought of everything. "Sure, I did homework on his computer. We were best friends. But that doesn't mean—"

"I'm not asking what it means. I'm telling you what Charlie said. He also claims he was home asleep the night you say you planted the bomb. His father agrees you never stayed over."

I was speechless again, but not surprised. I'd always known Charlie could do what he wanted, even make lies true. I'd even admired him for it. Mom moved closer to me, her hand on my shoulder. I said, "I was in the main building when the bomb was set to go off. I was right there. I'd have been killed, and Charlie was safe in a portable across campus. How much sense does that make to the police?"

Rossi looked down. "Yes. The police questioned him on that point as well."

"So?"

He rested his hand on the dirty sofa back, finding the words. "Charlie told them you were suicidal. He said a mutual friend had recently taken his life, and Charlie was trying to prevent your following suit. That he's sorry he didn't alert the school. But, of course, he never imagined you'd try to take others with you."

I yanked a hair from my own scalp. It hurt good.

Still, Rossi got me out of juvenile. Charlie was at the arraignment. He wore the same orange uniform I did, but in it, he looked small. He looked appropriately somber, too. Poor little Charlie, haunted by events beyond his control. But once, when no one else saw, I looked at him. And he smiled.

Rossi nudged me. "Stand straight!" he hissed.

When I looked again, Charlie had turned away. Big Chuck reached to pat his shoulder.

But he was in the hallway after. With his parents, glad he'd get to go home. I was going home too, but with a special ankle bracelet, a device that went off if I left our apartment or even stepped onto the balcony. I'd heard comedians joke about those things. Now, I was the joke. When we passed in the hall, Charlie leaned to whisper to his mother. She shrugged, and Charlie said, "Paul?"

I turned.

"I want you to know, I forgive you," Charlie said.

I didn't, couldn't speak.

Charlie looked at his mother, then made eye contact with me. "Sure. I mean, I don't know why you've chosen to victimize me, why you're saying these things." Charlie managed a tortured half-smile. "I thought we were friends, best friends. That's why I tried to help you. But the Bible says to forgive, and I do. I want you to get the help you need, Paul. And I want you to know there's no hard feelings."

I looked him in the eye and said the one thing I thought could hurt him:

"No, Charlie. There are no feelings at all."

Behind me, I felt Rossi, pushing me, grabbing my arm. We walked away, me feeling the ankle bracelet thumping on my leg.

CHAPTER THIRTY-SIX

They say I got off easy. My classmates' parents and even people I'd never met wrote letters to the *Miami Herald* demanding I be tried as an adult. Let the punishment fit the crime—which sounded like one of Reverend Phelps's sermons. After all, Kip Kinkel got more than a hundred years for those school murders in Oregon. The boys in Colorado got worse. They're dead. But no one died at Gate, and in the end, Charlie's mother's influence won out. I'm sure somewhere, Charlie's bragging about it, but I'm not there to hear.

No one understood why Mrs. Good helped me after what I'd done to Charlie. After all, I could have ruined Charlie's life or even gotten him kicked off the tennis team. Yet, she used her influence with the prosecutor to work a deal for me. "It was the Christian thing to do," she told reporters outside the courthouse. "Paul Richmond hasn't had the advantages my son has. I've always taught Charlie to pity those less fortunate.

I've taught him never to judge. Perhaps that explains their friendship."

But I know why she did it.

She came to see me after the arraignment. I was doing a jigsaw puzzle. Mom had bought me a couple dozen for Christmas. I'd already done them right side up. Now, I was doing them upside down—easy if you have all day. The court had arranged for me to take classes by closed-circuit television each morning, but it was two o'clock, and there was nothing on television but soaps. There was a knock on the door. I opened it.

"What are you doing here?" I stepped toward her. Her hand stopped me, reminding me of the ankle bracelet on my leg. I backed away before I set the alarm off.

"You're alone?" When I nodded, she walked past me into the room.

I followed, repeating, "Why are you here?"

"I can help you." I stared at her. She had blond hair and Charlie's eyes. "But if you tell anyone I was here, I'll deny it. And my help will go away."

That was like Charlie too. "Why would you help me?"

"Because you were my son's friend. Because—"

"Because you know he's lying?"

"What I know doesn't matter. Just listen to me."

I nodded.

"I have friends, powerful friends. They'll speak with the

prosecutor's office. They'll do what I ask. And you . . ." She stopped to meet my eyes. "You'll plead guilty and go to juvenile. Out at eighteen. The records can be sealed, and it will be like it never happened."

Except I'd lose two years of my life. But I said, "What about Charlie?"

"My son doesn't wish to testify against a friend. He'd prefer to forget the incident."

"Yeah, I'll bet he would."

The building was quiet. No one was there during the day. Everyone was at school, or working. Everyone except the losers with the ankle bracelets, which amounted to me. Had Mrs. Good timed her visit so we'd be alone? Of course she had.

"What if I don't plead guilty?" I asked.

"You'll be tried as an adult, tried for attempted murder. When convicted, your life will be destroyed. Forever."

"And Charlie? You're just letting Charlie get away with it?" I couldn't quite believe that.

"You're the one who confessed, Paul. A crime has been committed, and someone will pay. That someone will be you." She glanced at her watch, then stood. "I must go." She walked past me to the door, holding up her hand to remind me not to cross the line.

"Mrs. Good?"

She stopped, hand poised near the elevator button, so like

Charlie when he'd stood there weeks before. I remembered what he'd told me about Big Chuck then. The lies, the lies that were somehow true in Charlie's dark, twisted world. And I knew there was something I had to say—even if she wouldn't listen.

"I know what I did was wrong, really wrong. I probably deserve to go to Juvenile for it. I understand that now. But Charlie . . ." I don't even know why I bothered to say it. "You have to know Charlie was involved in this. It wasn't just me."

She tilted her head to one side, and I saw a flash of something—pity? No. Knowledge—on her face. She knew all about Charlie. She knew, but she wasn't going to do a thing. That was why Charlie was the way he was.

She smiled. "You've learned a hard lesson, haven't you, Paul?"

She took her hand away from the elevator button, deciding to use the stairs instead. I watched her from inside the apartment, standing there until long after she'd gone.

Classmates' Lives Take Very Different Courses

KEY BISCAYNE, FLORIDA— A local boy, Charlie Good Jr., shocked crowds at the Ericsson Open yesterday when he beat reigning Ericsson champion Peter Hofstedt 6–4, 7–6, 4–6, 6–3, in the semifinal round. He will meet John Gable in the finals tomorrow.

Good, 19, is a recent graduate of Gate-Brickell Christian School. This is the first time an unseeded player has ever reached the finals.

"It just shows that, with hard work and perseverance, dreams can come true," said Good's father, Chuck Good, wiping a tear from his eye.

In an ironic twist, one of Charlie's former classmates will be free to join in the rejoicing. Paul Richmond, nicknamed the "Brickell Bomber" for his unsuccessful attempt to blow up the exclusive school two years ago, was released from juvenile detention yesterday. It was his eighteenth birthday.

Followers of the case will recall rumors, spread by Richmond's defense counsel, that Good was involved in the bombing attempt. These rumors were vigorously denied by the Good family.

When asked to comment on his former classmate's athletic success, Richmond said he bore Good no ill will and was planning for his own future. "I realize now that I was responsible for my own actions. I hope that, in time, Charlie will learn the same. But I can't worry about him anymore."

Good had no comment on Richmond's release.

I write about the things that scare me. When I sat down to write my second novel for teens, I didn't have to go any further than the newspaper. Acts of violence in our schools are terrifying. What is it like, I wondered, to sit in class, not knowing whether the guy beside you might pull out a gun or plant a bomb? What is it like to feel you have reason to commit an act of violence at school—and nothing to lose?

I don't know the answers. But by writing the story of one teen who reached the breaking point, I've tried to make sense of something that teens are already trying to make sense of. I've tried to understand what makes some teens so fed up, angry, fearful, and—above all—isolated that they feel they must strike out. I hope this book will stimulate discussion. Although we cannot excuse the acts of kids like Paul, we must try to understand them. It is the first step toward preventing them.

Praise for BREATHING UNDERWATER

- **2002 Top 10 Best Books for Young Adults
  (American Library Association)**
- **2002 ALA Quick Picks for Reluctant YA Readers**
- **ABA Pick of the Lists**
- **Barnes & Noble Best Young Adult Books of 2001**
- ***Publishers Weekly* Flying Start**
- ***Bookselling This Week* Kids' Pick of the Lists**

"Alex Flinn's *Breathing Underwater* is the most challenging
kind of story, told from the most challenging point of view.
This isn't promising—it's promise fulfilled . . . beautifully
textured and detailed. It's a blockbuster."
—Richard Peck, Newbery Medal winner

"The situations and dialogue ring frighteningly true."
—ALA *Booklist*

"Beautifully told, with believable and
well-rounded characters." —*KLIATT* (Starred review)

"The messages in this unsparing novel of teenage love turned
dangerous are powerful. . . . This highly recommended book
should be required reading for all teenagers."
—*Voice of Youth Advocates*

F
FLI

Flinn, Alex.

Breaking point.

$15.95